The red door glared at me. I glared back and rapped on it. Louder I knocked, until I gave into pounding.

Then the frightening thought occurred to me that Spencer could have gotten into a car accident or something. He could be lying in some hospital, injured and broken, but how would I know? The folks at the school weren't talking. Mute language instructors. There's a new one.

I huffed, anxiety running its ruining course. Then I did something I'd never do under normal circumstances. I tried the knob. To my surprise, it opened.

Stepping inside, I said, "Hello," softly. "Anybody here? Spence?"

The silence I met caused me to slide further inward. The dull sound of particles shifting underfoot, as the rubber soles of my tennis shoes grated against something, caught my attention. I lifted my foot. That's when I noticed the shards of orange glass from a vase, which used to sit on the entry console table. It lay in fragments on the brown tiled floor.

My stomach did a flip. Proceeding into the main part of the house, the open kitchen and living room, I found things strewn everywhere, tipped over things, broken things.

Almost choking on a gasp, my hands flew to my mouth. "Oh my God," I mumbled, implementing an urgent plea through my fingers. "What on earth..." and then I think I had to pick my jaw off the floor, along with a framed photo of my brother with his beloved Ana.

Wings

THE UNSPEAKABLE

by

Tessa Stockton

A Wings ePress, Inc.

Suspense/Thriller Novel

Wings ePress, Inc.

Edited by: Jeanne R. Smith
Copy Edited by: Joan C. Powell
Senior Editor: Jeanne R. Smith
Executive Editor: Marilyn Kapp
Cover Artist:

Wings ePress Books
http://www.wings-press.com

Copyright © 2013 by
ISBN 978-1-61309-885-1

Published In the United States Of America

January, 2013

Wings ePress Inc.
403 Wallace Court
Richmond, KY 40475

"Forgiveness is the fragrance the violet sheds on the heel
that has crushed it."
                                                    Mark Twain

*"El perdón es la fragancia de los galpones violeta en el
                              talón
              que le ha aplastado."*
                                                    Mark Twain

One
Bogotá

My brother shifted in his seat. He picked his eyeglasses off the table before he set them down, *again*, for the umpteenth time. His nervous gestures began to irritate me.

"You shouldn't have come here," he said.

"Well, isn't that a nice welcome." I tried to bite back the hurt, but my voice sometimes does a quirky little tremolo that gives me away. I stared at the nearby palm tree, glad I came to Colombia, eager to explore its beauty. It beckoned, *Come, Sylvia, I will change your mundane life...*

If only Spencer caught wind of that sentiment.

He sighed. "Come on, Sylvia, I told you when you called a few weeks ago, that *now* was not a good time. You should have listened to me."

I had wondered when he'd start flexing his big brother muscles for-the-good-of-his-little-sister within our spanking new conversation.

"Spencer, I have vacation time overflowing. You know how it is. Use it or lose is. It's been six months since I've seen you..." I felt the tension spilling out as quickly as it came, "...and three months since I've had a *real*

1

conversation with you. We used to talk all the time," I whined.

He signaled for me to quiet down. "You're drawing attention. And stop gesturing with your hands so much."

I took note of his hand gesturing, and then glanced around the crowded outdoor café with a huff. "Fine. I'll try to be good." Usually rolling my eyes at him made him reach over in a playful manner and pinch my nose, an exchange we shared since we were kids. Yet, he sat oblivious to it this time. "Earth to Spencer..." He finally looked at me. "Are you feeling okay?"

"Yeah, why?"

"You seem, I don't know, distracted. And you're breaking into a sweat."

"No I'm not..."

"Yes, you are," I said, just as I watched him swipe a hand across his forehead and look at the sheen in his palm.

He shrugged, "It's hot today."

While the day foreboded a rise in humidity, Andean cloud forests kept the temperature poised, creating a perfect atmosphere that, if anything, I might consider a touch cool. "It's not that hot."

"It's hot." He gave me that do-not-cross-your-big-brother stare.

I rolled my eyes again just for good sibling measure, but met disappointment when he ignored that attention-hording attempt, too. "Then why am I not sweating?" I muttered.

"I thought you told me women *glistened* and not sweat...?"

I glared at my brother, feeling a tinge of sadness mingle in with the exasperation toward him. It didn't seem like the conversation was going anywhere. *Maybe I shouldn't have come here.* I snorted.

"What's so funny?"

"Not funny, Spencer, pathetic. Pathetic and sad."

"What's pathetic and sad?" he raised his brow.

"You are. We are." I sighed. "What's happened to you? We used to talk on the phone at least once a week when you first took this job here. I don't know if Colombia agrees with you."

He let out a long, almost painful exhale. "I'm getting another beer. Want one?"

"You know I don't drink."

"That's right." He snapped his fingers in mock remembrance. "Sylvia, the princess of prudence." He grabbed his eyeglasses and placed them back on his face, making a careful adjustment, and then stood. "Another Coke then?"

"*Síííí.*" I grinned up at him.

"Nice Spanish," he snickered. "You learned a lot since your last visit." He sighed. "Geesh. What are you doing here, Sylvia?"

"I told you."

Spencer ambled away under the veranda and came back with two bottleneck beverages, one in a puke-y brown colored glass, and the other in a clear glass with cool, refreshing black soda winking at me. At that moment, I could at least consider the cola my friend.

When my brother sat, the chair made a horrible screeching sound against the cement. He glanced around. "You remember this café?" He managed a smile, though it proved weak by any stretch. This was not the brother I knew...

"Yeah. You brought me here on my last visit, just before you took me back to the airport for my return flight home." I'm sure the smile I returned didn't inspire him any more than his did me.

He nodded. "Right. Back to the airport. Return flight home." He raised his eyebrows, suggestive of his forced will to send me away.

The urge to smack him overwhelmed me. I could feel my frown turn into a pout. I hated that, but couldn't seem to control it. I crossed my arms. "Now, you are *really* hurting my feelings. Maybe I *should* go back. Maybe I'll never see you again."

Spencer's brow furrowed. "Don't... geesh." He took his glasses off, rubbed his temples, the bridge of his nose, eyes clamped, before straightening his carriage and staring at me. "Don't say that." He suddenly reached for my hand across the round metal table.

A breeze wafted through the outdoor café, making goose bumps rise on my arms. I managed to catch the brochure on travel highlights in and around Bogotá I brought with me from the States, keeping it from flying away.

"Just...don't. Look. I'm sorry," Spencer said. "I'm glad you're here."

"You're not a very good liar."

"Sylvia, look," he barked, stopped, glanced around, lowered his voice. When he seemed to gain composure, he playfully tugged at my hand. "I'm trying, all right?" His voice came out little more than a harsh whisper.

"That's good. That's nice. Try to look happy to see me." That stupid tremolo again.

He leaned over the table, closer to my face. "Of course I'm happy to see you. You're my sis. We're close. I've always appreciated our friendship. It's just not a good time, you know. I just wanted you to wait until I could give you my proper attention, show you around, stuff like that. I'm preoccupied right now. There's a lot going on. Okay?" He expected an answer from me.

I pressed my lips together and nodded with acquiescence.

"Really?"

"Sure, Spence. Yeah, okay. I'll get a flight out tomorrow."

He groaned a sigh of relief and I saw the first real smile plaster on him since I arrived. "Great. I'll make it up to you, I promise."

"Right," I mumbled.

"And I'll get you into a good hotel for the night."

At that, I think my jaw must have dropped. Because he went on to explain without explaining. A bunch of jumbled words that had little value or meaning from a youngish English language teacher. Something about why I couldn't stay at his pad. I interrupted his pitiable justification.

"So what's the *real* reason, Spencer? You have another woman living with you again? Which one is it this time?" Did I really hear myself say that? I sounded like a jealous wife and not the man's sister. But he spoiled my feelings and the day in the beautifully contrasting city I desperately wanted to see! I wanted to get to know better the new and the old, skyscrapers amid ancient churches, the hectic pace of wide avenues with crazy drivers versus the peaceful paths for casual strolls, not to mention the vision of serenity the mountains to the east brought. I could see the line of mountains as I glanced from our table. They didn't bring serendipity, however. It, and everything, via Spencer, got the best of my nerves way before we sat at this nifty little godforsaken café. "Or are you still with that woman with five kids?" I blurted.

"Leave Ana out of this."

"Ah." I merely nodded my head. "So, it is still the one with the brood."

Spencer huffed as if he didn't want to admit it. "Yeah and so what? What's wrong with a lot of kids? I love kids."

"Nothing, only she's not a free woman," I chided.

"Her husband won't give her a divorce."

"It's not right, Spence. It's not moral."

"He's not a very nice man, to put it mildly."

"Still doesn't make it right." I looked at him. His lips pressed into a hard line, the tendon in his jaw pulsed. "I'm sorry. I had no right to say that."

"You're right, you didn't." He shifted in his seat. "For your information, I love Ana and want to marry her, but can't because of her spouse that *mother…*"

I held up a hand to impede him and he stopped. I hated cussing, and Spencer could navigate the alter language with a fleet of the world's very best sailors. In my good fortune, he often protected my ears from such things. Watching out for me, I guess. Although perhaps not so much on this particular day.

Spencer sighed. "It doesn't seem to matter anyway. Not with the way things are going."

"What do you mean, with Ana?" I was confused.

He scratched his head, the irritation of his mood pronounced in the action. "I'm in trouble, Sylvia." After staring into a distant nothingness, he finally met my focus. For the first time I noticed it. It's what seemed different about his appearance from the get-go. I just couldn't put a finger on it. His clear blue eyes reflected pain when they looked into mine. He was *scared*. I had never seen him scared.

"T-tell me..."

"I can't," he said, resolutely.

I shook my head, a prick of alarm slithering up my spine. My brother, always the happy-go-lucky type of guy...

"But *you* need to leave Colombia. Now. As soon as you can. It's not because I don't want to see you. It's just not safe." He stressed each of his words.

"Spencer. What is going on?" The demand in my voice came out too strident, but I didn't care.

This time he wagged his head. "Just, just trust me, okay?"

A slew of emotions flooded me. Upset, disappointment, anger, anxiety. Tears stung my eyes. "Fine."

"Okay," he stated rather than questioned, pleased to have won this tug-o-war.

I paused for a length before answering. "Yeah. Okay," I sniffed.

"You've got to be hungry, Sylv. Something to eat?"

I shrugged. "Sure."

"What would you like?"

"Well, since this'll probably be my only meal before heading back to Vancouver, I'd like that, what is it? I can't remember, *a-hee*..."

"*Ajiaco*. Good choice." He scooted out of his chair. "I'll be right back," he sang, as if we hadn't just had a conversation laden with all kinds of strange nuances. Spencer acted happy to get rid of me at least.

7

I thought about the stew or soup, whatever they referred to it, loaded with potatoes, corn, chicken, avocado, cream, yummy herbs. My stomach growled, remembering how much I enjoyed it during my last visit.

Rubbing the tension from the back of my neck, I didn't want to turn around and spend another fifteen hours on a plane, not to mention long layover intervals, flying back to Portland, Oregon, only to crawl back to my self-made dull life I yearned to escape in nearby Washington state.

I sighed and watched Spencer at the counter, ordering our food. While waiting, he fidgeted, paced within a two-step space, and rubbed his neck, too. What has gotten into him? In what kind of trouble could my brother possibly be? He worked as a linguist, for crying aloud. Then I thought of his girlfriend, Ana, a nice woman, petite. Young to have such a litter, I thought, but pretty—very pretty, in fact. I could see why Spencer was so smitten by her. Truly I could. And then it dawned on me that her abusive husband must have made some sort of threat. From what I understood, the man was capable of anything. Spencer was just trying to protect me, I mused. Prevent me from getting in the middle of things as I had often done.

Suddenly, along with a slight pang of guilt for my historical meddling, I felt bad for my brother, almost sorry for him. I didn't condone his involvement, his shacking up with a married woman, but under the circumstances, I understood the dilemma. Hers, especially...ruled by an abusive man, nowhere to go. A nice, stable guy comes along from another country and offers a safe haven along with his heart...not only for her but for her five children as well. It's a dream come true for Ana, really. No, I didn't condone the circumstances, but I understood. I even wished for a solution that seemed more... well... *appropriate* in the moral sense of the term.

Checking my cell phone for messages, I dropped it back in my purse with a sigh.

Spencer returned with two bowls of the thick soup and some bread. "Here we go... *ajiaco*. Enjoy."

"Thanks, Spencer." I grabbed the rim of one of the bowls and scooted it closer toward me, and then bowed my head for prayer to bless the meal. Discovering over the past few years that my brother really struggled with his faith, I didn't bother to ask him to join me in saying grace. His glance said it all. When I lifted my chin, I blew out a long exhale that somehow made it possible to fit in a genuine smile just for him. "Spence, I'm sorry."

"Huh?" He glanced up after taking a few slurping bites, chewing.

I shrugged. "I'm just really sorry I came here when you asked me not to. Sorry about my comments regarding you and Ana." I bit my bottom lip. "I don't ever want anything to come between us."

"And nothing will. You're my little sister. I'm your only brother. I'm just looking out for you." He reached over and squeezed my shoulder.

"I know. Thanks. Are we good?"

"Yeah, we're good." He sighed with relief. "I promise I'll call. When things clear, you can come out here for an obscene amount of time," he held his arms out wide, "and I'll make it all up to you." He winked and then pinched my nose.

Had I known that would be the last time I'd see my brother, things would have gone differently.

Two
Woman Trouble (Or So I Thought)

Almost as soon as Spencer helped me get settled in the hotel and arranged for my flight, he left, promising to pick me up in the morning to take me to the airport. We had no conversation together other than flight details, no exchanging of jokes, no brother hanging out with his little sister for an hour. Even a few minutes with him in the lounge, or room or lobby for that matter, would have been nice. He split, fast, leaving me standing outside my main floor hotel room with the door open, watching him scurry down the gold and brown-hued hall.

Spencer seemed nervous, as if he were late for some important speaking engagement. He couldn't wait to get out of there, away from me. With my mood spoiled, I sighed, stepped into my room, glanced around and peeked out at the adjoining courtyard through the back door. Finally, I shook out my balled fists, grabbed my purse and marched straight out of the room into the hall, locking the door behind me. If Spencer didn't want to spend time with me, fine! That didn't mean I had to stay staring at the four walls all night.

Coursing past the bottom of the curving stairwell, I headed through the lobby toward the main sets of double doors. Out on the street, I darted a step in each direction before pausing without an inkling of where to go or what to do. A passerby stared, craning his neck, even far down the street until he almost collided with a column of a building. There were parked cars. People sitting in parked cars. A couple ambled, holding each other close, whispering something to each other as they passed. I suddenly felt self-conscious. A breeze lifted my hair, the collar to my blouse. I hugged my torso and felt the sense of adventure slip from my system like water from a leaking pipe.

I about-faced and slipped back into the relative comfort of the hotel lobby, slinked down the narrow passageway to the lounge, sunk into a leather-padded chair, slapped my purse onto the table with a sigh and ordered a Coke. That much I could do without Spencer's assistance, although I felt strange and alone. My mind went blank as I took my time and sipped half the contents of my drink.

Two men entered the bar and sat in a darkened corner. To my relief, they kept to themselves. Although their eyes seemed somehow ambitious when we did catch eye contact on a few instances, perhaps roving, desirous for a glance at a woman who was obviously foreign, not to mention paler than the average gorgeous Colombian. Yeah, I stood out. Kind of like a blaring, neon sign that sometimes blinked.

No matter how much I loved the stuff, if I had any more soda I was going to pop. I pushed the glass away and stood, preparing to settle the bill, but the waitperson told me the nice men in the corner purchased my beverage. My heart flipped downward. *Great—just great.*

Now I have to go over there and pretend I appreciated the gesture, strike up some ridiculous small talk, when all I wanted was to retreat to my room and wait for daybreak to arrive so I could leave the hotel, leave the country I wanted to learn, leave my brother behind—just how Spencer saw fit.

I grumbled under my breath as I ambled toward the two men. This will not take long, I assured myself.

Shadows splayed across the men's faces. One stood and held the back of a chair for me. I noticed his hands. They were clean, nails trimmed and filed, immaculate. Donning a white sport coat over crisp jeans, this man was not a blue-collar laborer. Neither was the other, still seated, who also dressed above par.

"Oh, I can't stay," I said. "I just wanted to thank you for paying for my drink."

"*Por favor*," the man in white insisted.

"No, really. Thanks, though. You shouldn't have. Really," the word carried a drip of my annoyance.

The one still standing gestured to the seat, "Please, sit, please..." he motioned again, making it difficult to refuse.

With an inward sigh, I forced a polite smile and tentatively lowered into the chair. The man smoothed his white sport coat as he retook his seat. "Another Coca-Cola, perhaps?"

"What? No. Thank you. I couldn't finish the first one." When I grinned, the man returned the smile, while the other one, the one who had stayed seated, bore a face of stone. Yet, he possessed intensity in his eyes that went unrivaled.

"And what do you think of our beautiful city?"

I hate small talk. "It's fine." *I would have liked to see more of the city.* "Nice." *It's quite beautiful, what I've glimpsed.* "Beautiful."

"You like Bogotá?"

"Yes, yes," I smiled, trying not to sound condescending. "I like... Bogo... um, *me gusta Bogotá*," I said, while swinging a fisted arm for emphasis. Sort of like an aw-shucks or do-si-do to your partner.

"*Señor* Abbott... Spehn-sserr," the name danced on the Latin man's tongue. "He like Bogotá maybe too much, uh?"

I glanced back and forth between the two men with a deepening disquiet burrowing in the pit of my stomach. "You know my brother?" It came out more of a statement than a question. That's when I realized the speaking man put on joviality, while the silent man's intensity marked disdain.

This was not a chance meeting, and the conversation, though going nowhere, proved pointed. These guys had a problem with Spencer.

"Look," I said, "Is this about Ana—because, Spencer is really a good guy. He doesn't mean any harm, he's just...well, he's an idiot sometimes, but look, he has a great heart and he's just watching out for..." Words melted into oblivion just as soon as they tumbled out of my mouth.

The men took to their feet, preparing to leave. Not before the addressor leaned close to me with parting words, dripping syrup, "We will meet again, uh?"

Oh, I hope not. You're getting creepy. I delivered an award-winning smile to let them know I wasn't intimidated. I didn't realize until after they left the lounge that I had held my breath through that smile. *What was I thinking?* I asked myself when dizziness overcame me. Combine that sensation with a stomach bloated by too much carbonation, jetlag, mountainous elevation, and concern for my brother. It's a winning combination.

Spencer. I needed to call him and let him know about this little rendezvous. I didn't know what these men wanted. They appeared normal enough, but I detected the reek of dirty play.

"All about a woman," I muttered, searching for my cell phone. "When was the last time a man made a fuss about me?" Making a sound of disgust, I concluded, "How about...never."

"No?"

I noticed the waitperson standing beside me. He placed a glass back on the table.

"Oh, no, I didn't mean that."

"No?"

"No."

"Yes?"

"Yes, yes, you can take."

The glasses clinked when he picked them up with one hand; traces of residual amber liquid sparked through the transparency of one. I think the waitperson and I shared an expression of confusion, at least in our communication. Why hadn't I learned to speak Spanish like a good little sister and where did my cell phone go?

I dug through my overloaded yet bottomless purse. Finally, I turned it upside down, emptying the contents onto the freshly cleared table. Compact, lipstick in various colors, lip moisturizer, blush, eyeliner, mascara, gum, mints, the unmentionables (okay, things pertaining to feminine hygiene I quickly tucked back into my bag). Coins, hand sanitizer, antiseptic wipes, DEET (yeah, as if

I'm looking to go jungle-bound). More travel-sized items, such as mouthwash, tissues, toothbrush and paste, underarm deodorant (for the *glistening* woman), perfume (the cheap stuff), a pad of paper, pens, a pencil, fingernail clippers and Emory board. Small paperback (in case I get bored), crossword puzzle (in case I get bored), something else (in whatever's case), *additional* of something else...and all of this is more than anybody wanted to know, I'm sure. I patted my passport, which I kept on a sleek, beige money belt, along with my ID, debit cards and some currency. Anyway, I rummaged through so much stuff I almost forgot what I was looking for.

It wasn't there, my cell phone.

Drat.

I went to the front desk to call the café where Spencer and I ate earlier. Maybe I left it there. The only problem, I couldn't remember the name of the restaurant and trying to describe it to the concierge became a moot point.

Outside the lobby, night had fully descended. I didn't want to stand out there long in case Frick and Frack lingered nearby. Against my better judgment, I hailed a cab and instructed the driver, who steered the car swerving this way or that, attempting to lead him to find the café. After a few hit and misses, and occasional misunderstandings, a miracle! We located it.

"Wait here," I gestured with my hands. "Wait here for me, please... *por favor*," I said, well aware I spoke louder than necessary. The man wasn't deaf; I was dumb...to his language and his country—double dumb-dumb—especially taking into consideration that he understood English.

Scooting out of the cab, I glanced back twice to make sure he understood my intentions. I pressed down my clothes, more of a nervous gesture than the need to tidy, and squeezed between hundreds of micro parties under the veranda of the bustling café. The noise level high, I had to shout to a staff member dressed in a modish black shirt and apron.

"No. No phone left here, sorry. *Con permiso...*"

"Oh, sorry." I moved to let him pass, so he could deliver the tray of drinks he carried.

Close to the bar, I asked the one serving up concoctions. Like an octopus, his arms rotated everywhere, grabbing shot glasses, popping bottle caps, drawing from a tap, pouring, sloshing.

"*Con permiso. Con permiso!*" I butted in, but maybe I said it wrong or used it in an erroneous context. Giving up on the Spanish version, I shouted, "Excuse me." The bartender finally glanced up. I almost forgot what I wanted to say, "Oh, hi. Um, I was here earlier with my brother and I might have left a..."

"I do not know," he said.

" ...cell phone," I sighed.

"I do not know."

"You didn't even know what I was going to say," I said.

He shrugged, "I am busy, you see?"

"Yeah, right, I see that. Busy, busy." I turned with dejection.

A female server appeared from the back at a quickened pace. "I'm terribly sorry to bother you, but I..."

She bumped into me while hurrying past, and gave no indication she heard my voice. Under a different circumstance, I might have enjoyed invisibility.

I sulked.

There, the table Spencer and I shared earlier won my attention. Five people occupied it. For some reason, it felt as if I almost drifted toward it and stood staring down at it and its frame of people. I searched the tabletop, in case by some miracle the phone sat untouched. A few moments must have gone by when I noticed all five patrons stared up at me, with questioning amusement in their eyes. One of them said something. I shook my head, void of comprehension.

"You look for something?"

"A cell phone," I brightened, "have you seen it?"

"No. You left it here?" He used his hands as if in a karate chop.

"I'm not sure."

"To see it again, I think, chance is not good," he concluded.

"Great." This trip fast turned into a bogey.

"You would like to join us for a drink?" he asked.

My stomach distended a few inches from the earlier sodas, and I just wanted to get back to the hotel to loosen my belt, although the little group seemed very friendly. "No, but, thank you. *Gracias*."

The man expressed a touch of disappointment, and then, after a shrug resumed conversing with his companions.

Grateful to see my taxi still waited, I slid into the backseat and returned to the hotel. Turns out, Spencer put me up in one of the finest hotels in the area, according to the driver. Cabby must have commented, "Very, very nice, very nice" a dozen times, accentuating "very" a bit more each time he said it.

After settling the fare, which was not an easy task, for me anyway, I shuffled toward my room and inserted the key. A sigh of exhaustion caught in my throat when the door separated from its latch, as if not pulled taut. A common sense girl, I could have sworn I did the common sense thing and locked it before I left.

With hesitation, I pressed against the wood, opening it a little wider, wondering if I should call the hotel management first.

"Hello." I don't know why I said *hello* other than it seemed like the thing to do. "*Hola.*" *Hola* either.

I suppose I felt satisfied after peeking around corners and turning on all the lights that nothing went amiss. Nobody sprung out of closets or the shower, a pair of hands didn't grab my ankles from under the bed, pulling me off my feet. Imaginations still ran strong in my adult years. Crossing the room, I lifted the heavy, satiny curtain on the door that led to the semi-lit, vacant courtyard. It was a picture-perfect scene of serenity, complete with a fountain of gently gurgling water cascading down a three-tiered obelisk surrounded by palmed plants.

I cupped my chin and allowed my posture to slump in contemplation.

Ambling back over to shut and lock the door, I decided to dig for my pajamas; nothing like a nice shower and clean flannel to change into before bed. I zipped open my luggage and flipped over the lid. My cell phone lay on top of the pile, staring up at me.

Three
Brother, Where Art Thou?

Spencer had never disappointed me as he had on this morning.

The edge of the bed on which I sat sunk beneath my weight. I had an average build and heaviness. The mattress seemed to agree with my mood, not what I had for breakfast.

Having opened the door to the courtyard, a breeze wafted in, teasing my hair, twisting it around my face. Elbows on knees, I mindlessly passed my cell phone back and forth between my palms. I think at one point, or twenty, I glanced at it mysteriously, as if the little rectangular box contained secrets. Earlier I had a conversation with it, which included the accusatory "Where were you, I looked for you," and "How did you get in the suitcase? I don't remember putting you there..."

I sighed and motioned to punch in Spencer's number again, but somehow knew the receiver on his end would ring without end. Just like it had over the past hour.

With reluctance, I gained my feet, grabbed the handle of my luggage, and wheeled it, along with my purse, out of the room, shutting the door behind me.

Down at the front desk, they told me my brother hadn't left any messages. They directed me to the hotel's shuttle service to El Dorado International Airport. I boarded the van, hoping I'd still have enough time to catch my plane. The hour clamped down, narrowing those possibilities.

The ride to the airport made me nauseous. I can't say that traveling in the middle of such an amazing city and culture, transporting between unique architecture and history, the infrastructure didn't have its problems. Some of the roads were nice and expansive, but some needed desperate help. Both versions proved fully utilized and our twenty-minute drive took almost forty. I remembered this on my last visit.

Reminiscing over that time, I considered how Spencer and I had a much better experience then. It lasted only four days, but we still behaved, at least, in the context of a friendship, a sibling bond, we always found effortless between us. We had a lot of fun.

Sadness consumed me while musing over Spencer. He seemed lost, scared and confused. I missed my brother, the *real* Spencer...happy, joking, and carefree. He was always a little befuddled in the spiritual department, but I didn't give up hope and prayed for him until it became a ritual. In addition, he wounded my feelings. This went deeper than, say, a flippant comment would. My brother really let me down. I know I arrived in Colombia after he warned me not to, but I thought he'd forgive me over the fact that I missed him so much. It didn't seem to matter. Spencer was...*preoccupied*. I worried about him.

In some far-off fantasy, I hoped he made it through whatever made him late and waited for me now at the airport. After I lugged my stuff from the shuttle through the first set of doors, I knew that wouldn't be the case.

The airport was crowded; I flung my purse over my head and positioned it so that it crossed my chest diagonally, the weight of it pulling at my neck. I'd start to get a headache from it before long. Pushing through the crowd, I approached the gate for international flights. One last look around, anticipating Spencer, I moved toward the point of no return.

There was just one thing. I had a gnawing sense in the pit of my stomach. Even while he behaved abnormally, I still could not chew on the fact that Spencer stood me up. Yes, he was eager to see me go. Although hard for me to swallow, my return to the airport almost put a hop in his step. However, I couldn't come to terms with his absence just now. He wouldn't do this, I convinced myself. It's not like him.

Spencer could yell at me later.

I retreated through the masses and eventually found my way back to the transportation hub resembling a beehive. If only I were queen bee.

My imagination taunted again. It must have, because it seemed to take longer getting back to the hotel, even with the use of *Avenida El Dorado*, the acclaimed *fast* highway.

The familiar hotel's visage back in my scope, I shuffled to the front desk and asked for another room, a different one if they had it. They gave me the same one.

Still no messages from Spencer. I exhaled wearily near the counter. Sure, he'd display anger when I'd see him, because I didn't get on that flight as he told me to. But what was one more day? I'd arrange to fly out the next morning. At the very least, it would feel great to unload my luggage and purse.

I massaged the stiffening muscles in my neck and stretched my back before heading to my reassigned room.

This time when I called Spencer, the phone machine picked up instead of ringing continuously. "That's odd," I muttered, and then I listened to his recording. I decided to leave a message for him, even though I hate talking to machines: "Hi!...Spence!...Um, hey, don't be angry, okay, but I didn't see you this morning and I got worried. So...um...I'm back at the hotel." I clicked my teeth. "And I promise I'll fly out tomorrow, okay? Right now, I just want to know if you're okay. It didn't feel right leaving without seeing you, or at least talking to you. Call me."

With nothing left to do but wait, I explored the hotel, something I failed to do last night. It was elegant in its décor touched with the old world. I enjoyed traipsing the halls in which hung paintings of men on horseback in the midst of battle.

I discovered a reading room containing a small library. A middle-aged woman sat in a large wingback chair in the corner, her nose to a bind. I randomly selected a small stack of hardbacks with pictures and retreated.

Back in my room, I set the books down on the side table and flopped back onto the bed. I don't know if it was the unfamiliar surroundings, my concern for Spencer, or sadness over this hiccup in our relationship—because I don't usually like to nap—but I felt depressed and fell asleep.

I woke up to the phone ringing, but the sound came from the next room. Rubbing my eyes, I glanced at the nearby clock and then I yawned the twenty-minute nap out of my system. I pulled the stack of books onto the bed, mindlessly thumbing through them. Photos of enigmatic, untamed jungles captivated me. Gourmet food, colorful lights and dancing faces of Colombia. The pictures popped out in an amazing display, and I wanted to see and experience what the numerous photographers communicated through their work. Finally, in the last book I opened, a startling image made my stomach lurch.

"Oh, man," I muttered, ill prepared for the spectacle. A woman hovered like a ghost, her head fallen backward. She was strung up near the ceiling, hanging there, suspended. "What is this?" I said, scrunching my nose, flipping over the front cover to get the gist. The title read *¿Políticos Conducta?*

"Yeah, big question mark on that one," I breathed, while scratching my head.

I studied the photo of the woman again, bringing the page near my face for a closer examination. Underneath it, the caption read: *La violencia de las Américas.*

The victim's eyes and mouth were open in a strange manner. I could almost hear her terrible scream. Bloodcurdling, almost not human...like a banshee. For some reason, I tried to imagine myself in her place. I'm not a screamer. I wouldn't scream like that, I thought. I'm a silent sufferer. I'd probably writhe in agony, as agonized as this woman appeared, like her insides twisted outward until they burst, but I wouldn't give whoever would do something like this to another person the satisfaction of my scream.

I threw the book aside, my heart palpitating, almost thumping out of my chest. I stared at the ceiling. *That poor woman...*

I wondered what she did to get in that predicament. In what atrocious thing did she involve herself?

Another quick glance at the clock told me I had spent a half hour perusing the literature I brought back from the hotel's reading room, my inspection of the unprincipled photo monopolizing most of that time. The manifestation of that woman's suffering within my imagination during the last thirty minutes disturbed my conscience. She looked so weakened, terrified.

I'd be strong.

I sat upright, wiping sleep sand from the corner of my eyelids. In spite of an eerie sensation, and my concern over Spencer, my stomach nagged. It wanted food. I had a taste for more of that cheese, slightly sweet, unique to my experience in Colombia. Outstanding memories of the morning's *arepas* and hot chocolate I had for breakfast came to the forefront. *Feed the machine with more corn flour pancakes,* I thought. *I need fuel.* Then I'd track down Spencer to give him what for.

Four
Silent Treatment

Since my brother's house, located in the same district as the hotel, and a short jaunt from the school in which he taught, surfaced as number one on my list of possibilities for his whereabouts, I prepared for a little excursion in *La Candelaria*.

The sun warmed my back, and my comfortable tennis shoes cushioned my every step in the old downtown, past 400-year-old churches and through narrow streets lined with antique housing and museums. I felt Colombia underrated. It beamed and inspired, much more than any tour brochure or travel journal—as nice as they are— could possibly convey. One had to see it to imagine it.

True, outside news sources often relegated the nation by their concentrative stories of kidnapping, corruption and crime, rendered as the truest core of Colombian life. The result produced a negative image, but I found it rich with culture and dynamic, cheerful people. And I'm sure it was safer than the average person probably feared these days. Although, even Spencer warned I shouldn't go out after dark in the city, but I wouldn't do that in Vancouver. Every country, city, has its problems.

After strolling on part of a nifty bicycle route, I realized how turned around I must be. It seemed I headed back in the direction from where I came, instead of toward my desired destination. *Who needs maps? Well, I do, but it would also help if I understood them.*

I could do this all day—sightsee on foot—but I needed to get to Spencer's pad. Admittedly lost, I asked a kind passerby, but the elder, who was hard of hearing, didn't understand for what I was searching. However, he did point me to a small bus, a *colectivo*. On my last visit, Spencer and I took one to an artsy bohemian neighborhood, where we enjoyed true Colombian coffee at a distinctive little café. Huh, those were nice memories.

I fiddled with the bill of my baseball cap, ignoring my rising irritation.

In an attempt to ask the driver of a *colectivo* if his small bus would at some point intersect with my brother's neighborhood, he nodded with accompanying, "*Sí, sí*," before I finished.

"Okay, easy enough," I mumbled. Of course, I didn't know if the driver actually understood, or if he just wanted to fill his passenger quota for the hour.

There it appeared. Not five minutes later and the yellow language school where Spencer taught peeked through a barrier of green foliage. Trees, palms, shrubs and vine overgrown, covered the exterior in haphazard ways. It gave the institute either a forgotten look or one of exoticism.

I got off the bus early, explaining I had changed my mind and wanted to visit the school. After all, since Spencer didn't answer his phone, it's probable he had a class to instruct and right now stood in front of his attentive pupils. The driver tried to explain where the neighborhood was located from where we stopped, and I started recollecting my whereabouts. I knew I could walk the remaining distance to his house, at least. I thanked the bus driver quickly and he sped away.

Ascending a couple of stone steps, I peered through a panel of paned glass on a door ajar. I pushed on the wood portion of the entry, opening the door, widening it all the way with its hinges squeaking, alerting insiders that an intruder entered, or a late student anyway. I watched the back of a woman who didn't notice me as she disappeared down an adjoining hallway. A man standing at the front of the classroom stopped writing on the chalkboard and turned, his eyes behind his reading glasses squinting with scrutiny.

"*¿En qué puedo ayudarle?*" he said.

"I'll wait." I said, catching a hint of his inquisitiveness, yet not fully understanding. I gestured to a metal chair and sat in it, wondering why I didn't just hunt for the main entrance's information desk instead of disrupting the man's classroom.

The instructor shrugged and went back to writing. Then the man addressed the class speedily, apparently dismissing the students after pointing out an assignment on the board.

The students filed out of the room.

"Um, *perdón*, uh, excuse me, I'm sorry to interrupt," I said.

"*Sí,* and how can I help you, *Señora*...?"

"My name is Sylvia."

"Silbia?"

"Yes. I am looking for *Spencer Abbott*. He's one of the teachers here. Could you tell me where he is?"

The man's eyes flicked and turned back to the board. He grabbed an eraser and went at the chalk lines, expunging them, as if nobody's business.

"Um… I-I'm sorry… Spencer Abbott…do you happen to know which room is his at this hour?"

He said nothing.

"Hello… *hola*," My singsong came into play. "Spencer, well, he's my brother, would you…"

The man completely ignored me, turning his back every time I tried to make eye contact. It reminded me of some kind of keep-away game I played as an adolescent. His disregard started to irritate me.

"Excuse me," I said louder, cornering him. I grabbed the eraser from his hand. The man breezed by me and all but ran down the same hallway I saw the woman go earlier. I followed him. "Why won't you talk to me?" I demanded, a little less annoying than a little dog nipping at his heels. "I'm asking you a simple question. Hey!" The man swiftly turned and jogged up a flight of stairs. I stopped, aware of several sets of inquisitive eyes. I had found the lobby, at least.

One of these people had to know Spencer, or his whereabouts. I repeated my plea to locate my brother.

"Have you seen him? *Señor* Abbott…Spencer Abbott." Like a strike of lightning two women strode in opposite directions, disappearing in separate rooms. A tall young man tramped up a different staircase, skipping every other step. An ample woman in a bright pink dress stayed behind the semicircle desk, tidying stacks of papers. When I tried to talk to her, she shifted and started to fill a stapler with staples. The lines in her forehead knitted together; even then, I could swear she looked anxious.

As a youngster, I always liked *The Twilight Zone*. I found it both spooky and interesting. Never thought I'd actually step into one, but this scenario at the language institute proved spooky and interesting.

"Yeah," I tapped my knuckles on the counter, "thanks," I muttered, crestfallen and perplexed.

Do you know how maddening it is when everybody around you ignores you, practicing silence when you need to have answers? I had a simple question: have you seen my brother? They had the simplest of answers.

Can you hear the crackling of an old record spinning on a player? The kind of silence when all that's missing is a screech as the needle drags across the vinyl. Yeah, that was coming.

I left the school from the main lobby, made passage around it as if I, Joshua, circled the walls of Jericho. With the school relatively small, it didn't take long. Besides, neither did I go around seven times or make noise.

Back to the lobby's entrance, I shoved off to find my brother's house, address penned on a piece of paper in hand. Glancing back over my shoulder, I witnessed several sets of curtains on the upper level that shifted a smidgen, as if invisible eyes had peeped through a second ago. The fabric swayed slightly, waving back into place.

"Peekaboo," I said, sarcasm getting the best of me. I added a wave for good measure, just in case they didn't notice I noticed. However, take note, if you are ever traipsing a fifth dimension, don't wave or practice sarcasm. Don't ever let them know you know. It comes back to bite you.

Down cobblestoned backstreets, I finally found my brother's small blue house tucked away in a row of other colorful houses. Like the school, a wall of green foliage wrapped around the entrance, like tentacles. I stepped under an arbor, thickened with plant growth since my last visit, to the portico. The red door glared at me. I glared back and rapped on it. Louder I knocked, until I gave into pounding.

Then the frightening thought occurred to me that Spencer could have gotten into a car accident or something. He could be lying in some hospital, injured and broken, but how would I know? The folks at the school weren't talking. Mute language instructors. There's a new one.

I huffed, anxiety running its ruining course. Then I did something I'd never do under normal circumstances. I tried the knob. To my surprise, it opened.

Stepping inside, I said, "Hello," softly. "Anybody here? Spence?"

The silence I met caused me to slide further inward. The dull sound of particles shifting underfoot, as the rubber soles of my tennis shoes grated against something, caught my attention. I lifted my foot. That's when I noticed the shards of orange glass from a vase, which used to sit on the entry console table. It lay in fragments on the brown tiled floor.

My stomach did a flip. Proceeding into the main part of the house, the open kitchen and living room, I found things strewn everywhere, tipped over things, broken things.

Almost choking on a gasp, my hands flew to my mouth. "Oh my God," I mumbled, implementing an urgent plea through my fingers. "What on earth..." and then I think I had to pick my jaw off the floor, along with a framed photo of my brother with his beloved Ana.

Don't ask me how, but a feeling had already come over me, a certainty that led me to believe nobody lingered in Spencer's house, waiting to inflict harm from the shadows. I suppose I wondered if I'd find my brother in his bed, lying in a pool of blood.

I witnessed none of those things. In fact, other than objects, files, cabinets ransacked, and the occasional broken glass, no Spencer traces existed that I could see. I'm not even certain there proved signs of struggle between one human and another. It didn't even look like a robbery because I noticed items present, sitting stationary and quiet that *I* would have taken had I been a thief.

It appeared as if someone searched for something, though.

I proceeded with caution until I had just about enough.

Still holding the framed picture of my brother and Ana, I noticed a small crack through the lower left hand corner of the glass. Carefully, I removed the photo from the frame and slipped the recent shot of Spencer in my purse.

I didn't waste time in scurrying over to the neighboring houses to ask if they'd seen anything, heard anything, if they knew *something*.

An old man, who gardened the tiny patch in front of his pinkish house with bright blue shutters, and who stared at me when I first got to Spencer's, turned his back before I reached him. I watched the old man hobble inside even as I shouted. Moving around the fence line and marching to his door, I pounded. Rude, I know, but desperation began rearing its head in intolerable measures.

The other nearby house was next on my list, and the one next to it. I received the same treatment, either ignored or unanswered. Yet a familiar quiver of fabric waved to me from the inside of some of these homes.

Eyes, all eyes, watched. This could not be the Colombian way, I thought. The people seemed too gregarious to hide and disregard others as they have me. What happened to the warm and lively Colombians Spencer fell in love with? "Come out, come out, wherever you are," I muttered.

My next option: contact the authorities. I hoped then I could get some assistance. Did I mention the police in Bogotá had a reputation?

Five
A Squad Car Named Desire

The sun began dropping, quickly, from the skyline. I waited for nothing, even after numerous calls.

"Please, can you send somebody?" "Get here quickly." "I've been waiting forever" and the favorite I thought would generate enthusiasm, "My brother has gone missing."

When considering the sizeable number of kidnappings the country experienced—at least reported by those outside news' sources I mentioned earlier—it wasn't difficult to understand the lackluster response to my telephone report. It's just...well...it's different when it's your own flesh and blood. Sounds self-centered, I know, but I honestly don't know how anybody could behave differently.

And no, the city police did not, to my knowledge (and I admit, that's limited), have a reputation. The drug cartels and guerrillas did. However, I pronounced one for the police, right then, right there.

Oh, once something that resembled an unmarked squad car, much akin to an old Ford Falcon some governments in the southern cone once favored, inched by. I watched it, with the three men inside, staring. My heart pitter-pattered with relentless hope, the teasing fingers of relief toying with my spirit.

Alone, I so longed for help; any assistance would do, even this masked auto. But when I approached it, the vehicle accelerated. I ran after it, arching my arms in frantic semicircles. The brake lights lit.

"Oh good," I whispered like a perfectly normal maniac. I slowed for a second, the light green hunk of metal close, almost within reach. I proceeded.

So did the metal on wheels, zipping from sight. Red taillights disappeared. The unofficial official car danced around a corner—gone.

Tease!

Six
Another Dimension

The temperature dropped. I hadn't brought a sweater and shivered in the newfound cold. Strangely, the street remained vacant of pedestrians, and nobody came to or went from their houses. It was as if The Plague ran rampant, people scurried in fear, and I was the plague. Yet, I still stood there, unintentionally affecting such a pretty setting.

I had gone back and forth from inside Spencer's house. Don't know why. To find a link somehow, to pretend I didn't just see the aftermath of his house rummaged. It was an act of denial, I suppose, for someone a little on the sensitive side.

Well, the local police had given me a tip of contacting the U.S. Embassy at least, which meant they decided not to help me. I really don't know why I didn't think of it earlier. That's what a foreign traveler is supposed to do in cases like this, but I wanted to get somewhere more public before night closed in. If in the right frame of mind, I would have appreciated the beauty, the sky that turned a vibrant orange, reflecting off old buildings amid new, enveloping in richness, all the colors the city displayed, the fragrances, the light breeze, even if I didn't run myself in the ground with worry and an empty stomach and clammy skin.

When passing a narrow, brick alley, between rows of houses, I jumped a mile (or so it felt) when someone slammed a window. Nearby, another door shut. I wondered if this section of town got the memo that I was coming through.

Ah, a plaza! A big, gorgeous, secure area where night lovers lingered, completed with fountain, benches, cobblestone, and illuminated by quaint lampposts. Sweet! I stumbled on it by accident, or perhaps, God heard my pleas for just this kind of thing and decided to grant provision.

I stopped, closed my eyes for a moment and sucked in a large lungful of air.

Nearby, boys gave llama rides to tourists. Although night descended, I had a feeling the llamas would remain there on the tiled plaza floor until the very last tourist left. Business was looking good for the lads. For a second, I forgot everything and smiled back at one of the handsome youngsters much too young to operate a business, in my opinion. I wondered where they lived, if they had parents, did they go to school, is this what they did to survive or to provide entertainment.

A guitarist strummed his guitar, crooning to those who passed by. He nodded to me with a smile and a wink. A table of college age students sitting at a café table near the street musician began singing along with him. People enjoyed themselves. The air filled with excitement, the good kind. Like a salve, I soaked it in, and wound my way to another café. Its door open, music of a different kind drifted out to meet me. In some ways, I felt strange, numb, and only went where my feet took me. For some reason, they took me here, inside, where a woman sang a soft Latin ballad...jazzy, my pacifier.

I slid into a small red leather booth where I ordered food. Three men next to me argued amiably over coffee and cookies sprinkled with coconut. Once, they tried to draw me into their conversation by exhibiting broad, gracious smiles and inviting me in English. I shook my head, appreciative but indecisive, confused and distressed. They had kind and inviting faces, yet I tried to ignore them. Huh, I guess the coin had turned since my visit to Spencer's language school as well as his neighborhood.

My food came after my third call to the embassy. Referred to Chuck Goren, I left him messages. Apparently, he was out. I called again, explaining the situation to the receptionist. She said she'd transfer me to another person, but I got Mr. Goren's machine again. I started to leave another, angrier message, but this time the receiver picked up, I heard his voice on the other end.

"Ms. Abbot—Sylvia, is it?"

"Yes."

"Can you come and meet me here first thing tomorrow morning?"

"Are you kidding?"

"Yes, well no, I'm not kidding. How does tomorrow morning look?"

"I'm not trying to get in to see a doctor, Mr. Goren. My brother is missing! The inside of his house is in ruins. I don't know where he is. I'm worried about him. Can't you do something, *now*?"

"Nope. Budget cuts, we're understaffed..."

I pulled the phone away from my ear and shook it. Then I cupped it against the side of my head again as if that solved everything and I'd get a different rundown this time.

"...understaffed, budget cuts..."

Resisting the urge to chuck my phone, I gritted my teeth before I also enacted a battlefield scene with my plate of *Carne en Polvo*.

"Mr. Goren," I interrupted. "My brother is apparently in some sort of trouble. My feeling is that this has to do with..."

"Ms. Abbott. We are dealing with a... a... *situation* here."

"What situation?"

"We've received another bomb threat."

"Oh my goodness," I whispered.

"It's close to elections, politicians are politicking. Happens all the time. Most of the threats are false. We'll do our routine scouring, and then be back to normal. So, Ms. Abbott, tomorrow sounds...?"

"Good."

"Goodnight." He cleared his throat. I imagined he loosened a necktie ahead of hanging up.

"Well, isn't that nice? This can't be for real." I attacked my meal—meat, sauce, tomatoes, beans, rice, and loads of garlic—digging into it but not really tasting it. Beside myself, I wolfed it down in five minutes. All to the surprise of the three amigos, who ceased their heated debate long enough to watch me down my food as if a performance in a circus act.

Didn't drink anything—hadn't had a beverage since lunch. My throat parched, I felt the repercussions of the day's dehydrating stress but didn't care.

After settling the bill, I called for a taxi service and waited across the plaza by the statue where the company informed me the ride would come. It came quickly. I gave the driver the last two digits of my phone number...a key code, I guess, to make sure I was a legitimate customer. He wanted to chat; I didn't. In a peculiar way, I would have felt more comfortable with the language institute inhabitants on this night, you know, the silent ones who taught others how to talk.

At the hotel, I checked for messages at the front desk in case Spencer called. Maybe he was with Ana and they got caught up in something trivial, and his messy house proved another incident entirely. In fact, perhaps Spencer wasn't even aware of his house. Wouldn't that be great? He would call and I could warn him.

I entered my room quickly, shutting and locking the door behind me and then glanced at a mirror. Large wet splotches soaked obvious parts of my shirt. Pit stains.

So much for glistening...

After a shower, I threw on another tee-shirt. It felt too hot to wear pajamas. I crawled into bed draping an arm over my eyes, completely spent. It was quiet. The only sound in the room seemed to come from my gurgling stomach.

Images raced through my head like some sort of fever-induced drama. I felt so unsettled. Finally, I fell asleep, but it didn't last long. Maybe if I weren't such a light sleeper it wouldn't have happened. I'd still be safe.

Seven
The Force

In the chaos of a restless night where alien images of a nervous Spencer stabbed my conscious and unconscious moments, I sat up with one final gasp. The toilet began running as if the tank decided it hadn't filled with enough water, and then the sound of soft scraping drifted all the way through the outside door like it was a piece of onion paper.

A troubling feeling washed over me. A different noise from the hall made me jump. I found my feet in no time. Using my hands to comb back my damp hair, I grabbed a long robe in the closet and tied it around the tee-shirt that hung off me.

The taps of whoever knocked on the hotel door remained quiet, yet even.

I looked through the peephole and recognized a vest with the hotel's name embroidered on it. The steady taps from the man on the other side of the door echoed against the chambers of my bosom, until I blew an anxiety-filled puff of air and unlocked the deadbolt.

Opening it with a determined swoosh, I gripped the door and said, "Yes?"

"*Señora* Abbott?"

"Yes."

"My apologies for disturbing you at this late hour," he gave a slight bow, "however, there is a man who is here who says he is your brother..."

"Spencer?" I clasped my hand around my throat in hopeful angst.

"A *Señor* Spencer Abbott—*sí*, that is correct."

"Where?"

"If you will follow me," the man executed another small bow while taking two steps backward. "He did say it was of...an urgent matter."

I didn't even close the door fully or put my slippers on. Barefoot, I followed the man down one hallway after another. I recognized a kitchen through the square window of a swinging door, dark, save for a dim light over the industry-sized sink. We passed a small room full of cleaning products, another with white linen and towels piled up next to a line of washers and dryers. All was silent, everything resting for the night.

"Forgive me, but where exactly is he?"

The man hesitated and then the corner of his mouth inclined. "We have a waiting room in the back...for after hours, you see. The entrance to the front lobby is closed at night." He motioned his head toward the direction from which we came.

"Ah," I nodded. "Makes sense." I smiled, nervous yet thrilled for the chance to talk to Spence again.

The hallway narrowed. I couldn't get to my brother fast enough and practically tripped on the hotel employee's heels. He pushed open another door and I thrust through ahead of him until I realized I exited to the outside, my feet clapping against abrasive cement. I froze. The click of the door sounded as it shut. I whirled

41

around. The man who removed his embroidered vest crossed his arms.

"What…"

I couldn't get the question out. My voice stammered.

Something was happening to me, some sort of delusion?

Fear rose up. A sensation increased until I knew for sure someone yanked my head back by a fistful of hair.

I tried to cry out, but something blocked my lips from parting.

What little I could see in the night suddenly dimmed. Something covered my head, my face. I tried to pull it off. Then I felt my arms wrenched toward a powerful magnet, my back, where they stuck there like superglue, bound.

I couldn't see, but a force propelled me forward. My shin caught something hard. My toe stubbed. I fell but couldn't catch my fall. That same force had me on my feet again.

Jesus. What is this? Wake me now! Delusions, go!

Wind against my bare legs. That's when I realized I lost the robe somehow.

The force pushed me into a car. The trunk, I think, because it felt too enclosed. I've never liked tight spaces. Spencer used to tease me about claustrophobia. *Spencer, what is happening?* The scream reverberated in the confines of my skull. Then I heard muddled voices coming from another compartment.

I tried to kick, but with bare feet, I only stubbed more toes. I might have even broken one.

Cinched back so tight, my arms began to ache. The feeling of suffocation came on me in overwhelming proportions. Beads of sweat formed. I couldn't move my mouth. The thing over my head blocked sufficient airflow. I felt sick to my stomach. My heart pounded. What if I had to throw up, I wondered. The gag over my mouth wouldn't let it come out. Would I choke? I needed to use the bathroom.

The vehicle stopped not long after. My breathing quivered, body trembled. The large number of quick swallows reverberated in my head. Everything uneven, unsteady, the wrench from the trunk catapulted me to the ground, face down on concrete. I groaned, but even that was stifled.

Another pull of the hood and my head jerked back so far I thought I broke my neck. On the feet, on the double, the force shoved me forward. Seconds later, the sounds of the city disappeared.

Stairs. Descending now…

Tripped up, hard soles crushed my bare feet. I fell down several sets of steps. I was caught, but not without the hard introduction to a wall.

Downward again, the temperature changed. It felt dank. Then, what I couldn't smell before, I smelled now. A horrid odor, a mixture of nasty human secretions, filmed my nose, my throat. My stomach flipped. I could barely contain my urge to gag, to heave. The smell of urine, feces, and vomit thickened the air, creating its own sort of humidity. At the same time, the force pushed me into a chair. It tipped, we fell, the chair and I. The force reversed the motion, flipping us upward, strapping us together as one.

Then I could see light. My hood came off.

A bright, intrusive shaft flooded my face. I squinted against it, and while my eyes tried to adjust to the unadjustable, in the exterior dimness, what surrounded me belonged in something like a little shop of horrors. Yes, that was it. I was in a movie, in a formulaic interrogation scene. But...*how*? Just how did I get to play this actor, and when would the picture end? How much would I earn for my performance?

Jesus.

One could hardly detect the pastel-painted walls beneath the coating and ceiling-high splatters of blood, humans' vital substance. Would mine soon join the mural?

Since the force removed my hood, they had to remove the duct tape, too. Otherwise, how would I answer the questions I didn't know they'd ask and I didn't have answers to? I had wondered if I still owned two whole lips, but the musing didn't last long.

In the diffused light, I witnessed several sets of heads. The heads didn't move for the longest time. It was as if I were a subject to study, like a chimpanzee, for the heads to learn about my intelligence or reactions and to take notes.

The anxiety the moment created just about killed me. That was before I learned about the other things that could kill me.

Finally, a man stepped forward in methodical footsteps, one excruciating step after another. The light shifted and I could see him better, first his green pants, then the pistol at his side and finally his face.

Frack.

Yes, I recognized him, one of the men who paid for my soda at the hotel bar, the quiet one with the heated eyes. But where was his counterpart, Frick? My eyes scanned the various heads. Definitely not bobbles.

I glanced at him again, Frack. It was there that I got sick. It lurched out of me, landing on his boots in a kind of lumpy mess. They just lost their shine. I suppose he stood there assessing me when my last meal before my capture came up in violent revolt, a reaction to the fear I tried to control, yet failed miserably, as miserably as I felt. I couldn't even wipe my mouth because my wrists remained tightly bound. Have you ever tried that—vomit without the ability to move a single extremity? Anyway, right after I spewed, with trepidation I dared raise my gaze to meet the return glare of my teed-off oppressor.

There expended a brief pause, which I relished, before he sent us (chair and I) flying with a blow to the side of my head (lucky chair).

Back in place, I roused to the sensation of sharp tapping on my cheeks.

"Wake up, *señora*. We have work to do."

I groaned.

"Do not waste our time."

I groaned again.

More tapping came, harder, more like slaps. I opened my eyes.

"Name?" he demanded.

This marks the beginning of the extent of the names exercise. Your name, his name, her name, their name, give us a name, pick a name, enough with the names…"Leave me alone," I mumbled.

I had no idea what these people wanted. Didn't have a clue about what they said.

Their questioning grew relentless, brutal. Noticing early on that it didn't seem to matter, my answers, I did something I normally didn't do. Life's circumstances flipped on me. In a moment, I crossed over some kind of threshold where nothing made sense. So—*Lord, forgive me*—I lied. I made one up, threw one out there, a name, and hoped they'd stop. But the only thing I could think of came from something I'd seen from a Seinfeld episode, a story of a fabricated boyfriend of Elaine's, a matador named, "Eduardo Corrochio." The comic scene made me laugh then. I rather chuckled now, too, under the watchful gaze of my interrogators, but delirium had already set up camp.

A nod from Frack and feet shuffled. Several of the heads actually did bobble then. Those same heads departed.

"You tell us the truth, *señora?*"

I nodded to the sound of another voice that came out of the shadows. *Ah, Frick! There you are, you rascal.*

"If not, you will pay." He stroked my cheek in an intimate manner. Put his thumb in my mouth until I choked.

I hated this the most, the sexual elements to my torture.

Then sometime after my introduction to *la picana,* the cattle prod, where Frick and Frack worked faultlessly together, one adjusting, the other administering, applying it to my most sensitive body parts, the others returned with a poor young fellow, probably just a teenager, on whom I unknowingly ratted. A modern day Eduardo Corrochio—he actually exists. I never would have thought.

"Thassnothim," I said, against a swelling tongue.

"What did you say?" Frack asked.

"Wwong guy." I struggled to breathe against the tightening in my chest.

46

"Are you sure?" Frack cocked his head. However, the way he did so made me think he didn't intend to change direction. Maybe the tilt of his mouth gave it away, the sneer.

Frick, the one who thought he deliberated better with his pants off, closed in. "You must not lie to us, pretty one, especially to Puma, here," he said, gesturing to Frack. "He is a predator and do you know what predators do...?" He straddled me, his mouth almost upon mine. "They kill," he whispered, and then he smothered me.

"Come, let us do this thing, finish this business." Frack, who became Puma, at that point, spoke up, urging his friend who, at last, retrieved his tongue from my throat. Puma stared. I remember thinking his face did rather resemble a cat's.

They started Eduardo's session right in front of me. *Oh, God, what have I done?*

"No-no-no, lied, I lied, made up hithname, thop, pleathe!"

"*Si.* You lied. So we are teaching you a lesson. Maybe next time you will not lie to us, uh?"

They fulfilled their commitment and carried through. That poor soul...all my fault, I thought. "God forgive me," I whimpered.

"Ah! No, no, no," Frick exclaimed, wagging his finger. "*We* are god here, *señora*, and *you...* you are nobody, nothing. No one will rescue you here. Your prayers go unheard. Here, we are god. Welcome to my kingdom." Frick laughed in his glory.

I'm not sure how much time passed, but another set of arms loosened the tethers, dragged me out of the room, down a hall into another narrower hall shut off by a pair of doors and dumped me. I could barely move, let alone walk, yet they joined my ankles and wrists with chained cuffs much too tight. The cuffs dug into my flesh, but I welcomed it. I'd welcome anything after electric shock.

They removed my clothes at some point early on. I don't even recall the incident. Yet, now I experienced shame when the eyes of others like me, who I knew had gone through what I just had, sized up the new addition to their crammed corridor. An area sectioned off, it formed a makeshift jail. People sat or had passed out, depending on the amount of time since their last session, and the severity of it. Whimpering moans of pain drifted. I unwillingly joined the cacophony.

A moment later, guards came in and grabbed a man by his ankles. He hollered all the way down the hall. You'd think the farther he traveled, the fainter the noise would get, but it proved the opposite. His screams reverberated down the halls, echoed off walls, sliced through my dulled ears and heightened our fear. The whimpering and moans increased, too, as did the numbers who cried.

I slid my arms up, cold chains dragging across my chest, until I had covered my head. Unbearable, and yet impossible to escape. *Lord Jesus, can't you hear this?*

Previous words clanged in my mind in ruthless circles, "We are god here, and you are nobody."

"Not true, not true, not true," I tried to speak in my state of disorientation, but no sound came out.

My arms yanked upward by the chains, I roused to panels in the wall whizzing by. I must have fallen into some sort of stupor, because I don't remember them coming and dropping off the man whom they had just broken to swap for me. I couldn't even prepare for the second session, mentally, physically, emotionally, spiritually—just like the first time.

Round two of torture stretched into an even worse scenario. The questions deepened, changed. Of course, they wanted names, always the names, but this time they demanded to know why I came to Colombia. They made it clear I wasn't welcome. I think they called me a subversive parasite, and accused me of contaminating their country. I remember one's impassioned words, "You are a plague-ridden rat." He spat in my face. "If you do not cooperate and tell us what we want to know, I will force this rat poison down your throat." He picked up a box and shook it. I found the sound of pellets rattling inside a half-empty box effective.

"I jutht came to eat a bowl of *ajiaco* with my brother." It sounded innocent enough, the truth. I think they thought I used sarcasm, and I paid for it when they doused me with water. It intensified the shock.

I will never eat *ajiaco* again.

They asked me about my brother, Spencer. I was surprised. I told them he was an idiot in love, who didn't want me to interfere with his relationship; that his girlfriend had a jealous husband. I said to them that Spencer told me to go back home to North America. And how sad it made me feel that he didn't want me around. I only stayed because I discovered his house broken into. Once I saw to my brother's welfare, I planned to leave, I assured them.

The silence that ensued drove me mad.

"I jutht want to make thur he'th okay."

All I could hear was the unremitting drip of water. The stillness broke when Puma approached and attacked me with fury. Then he froze, as if he considered for a

49

second what he was doing. He raised his hands and backed up into a table, knocking tools of the trade over onto the floor. They fell with a strangely harmonious clatter. He turned, grasping his wavy hair, and sat in a chair with his back to me, slumped over, rocking as if in pain.

I don't know how I could witness all this. I suppose the swelling hadn't puffed up that bad yet.

Frick prattled something to him impatiently. I imagined something like, "Get a grip, you are displaying weakness."

"*Sí, El Capitán*," I heard Puma wheeze.

They exchanged a more detailed conversation then, feeling the liberty, figuring I really didn't understand Spanish. Much about me they learned in that timeframe, especially my weaknesses. I didn't know I had so many.

Frick neared me. He reminded me of a slithering snake. I wondered what moniker he used. Snake was apropos, geoduck (gooey duck clam) fitting, and something I imagined straight from my brother Spencer's vocabulary, horse's ass—bingo! My mother would wash my mouth out with soap on that one, but apparently, right now, I have no mother, father, brother, or god. I am nothing, so he has said while sharing the sentiment among his *compañeros*.

I must have passed out, because the next time I gained consciousness, they pulled me from the stuffed jail floor to which I don't remember returning. And my eyelids had sealed shut from the swelling, so I couldn't watch the wall panels go by on my magic slide down the hall to that vile room I learned was referred to as their "operating theater."

After several more sessions comparable to the first, in fact worse, I thought it would never end. Time blurred. I didn't know if I struggled to exist under their tyranny for hours, days or weeks. Begging for mercy was out of the question. The names bit, a regular part of every interrogation, was a moot point. I didn't know how I got there in the first place or why, but in the recesses of my teetering mind, I asked God, in whom I *believed* I still believed, to rectify the circumstances.

Then, something transpired quickly, a drastic change.

Eight
Transport

At the mercy of the godless kingdom and under the rule of the godless gods, I would embrace any kind of alteration to the circumstances they offered. However, weakness settled so deeply in my bones that expression, other than the newfound screaming-like-a-banshee part, grew dormant.

That woman in the photograph within the pages of the hotel's book...she flashed in my mind. I understood her plight. And we screamed the same, she and I. Weak, strong, it didn't matter anymore.

My transition from A to B would make anybody cringe. I have no ego left, only shame and embarrassment. With hoods pulled over our heads once again, they herded us into another area, the chains clinking and scraping against the floors as we moved like cattle. The thick dragging sound had to belong to those who were still unconscious, tugged by their limbs.

A woman's panicked scream ricocheted, and soon all our voices rose up. All of us chosen for this transfer anyway.

"They plan to kill us, they take us somewhere to murder us," a man shouted in English for my benefit. I've once heard ignorance is bliss. I think it might have been true in this case. My body may have been broken, but I discovered at that exact moment I still had the resolve to live.

An eruption of batons began striking after we were ordered to silence. I was one of the few who obeyed and remained quiet, yet I took a blow to my skull.

My head throbbed. Every inch of my body ached. My eyes felt infected beneath the hood. I needed water! I was so thirsty. On top of it, the more I roused, the more I detected a horrible stench. *Ugh, what is that smell...*

I felt something sticky underneath me. That's when I realized where the odor came from. I had involuntarily defecated.

Blind, naked bodies pressed against mine, jostled by the motion of a vehicle. We all sat in the back of some sort of truck expelling diesel fumes. No room for modesty here; I was growing numb anyhow.

Not knowing how long I had lost awareness, how far we had already traveled; it seemed we'd never stop. Someone in the truck retched, and another person thereafter. One could no longer hold his/her urine. Everybody feared asking the force operating the vehicle to use the bathroom, and so released on themselves or others. The reek filling the space around us became unbearable, and yet, there we were, tolerating it. We had no choice.

The roads grew bumpier, winding. We could hear the gears of the truck grinding as the driver shifted up and down. We ascended for a time, the truck stopping and inching as if maneuvering around a mountainous cliff-lined road. *Good grief, where are they taking us?* Then the descent came, much quicker and smoother, until a large, unexpected pothole sent us flying, one over the other. I felt parts of bodies I didn't want to feel and retracted as fast as a near-broken body could.

Running my tongue over my sore gums and teeth, my mouth felt like cotton. I had a yearning for water that bordered on desperation. During the sessions, a medical doctor sometimes poked in to check my vitals. His job to keep me alive in order to sustain the duress of torture seemed such a paradox. Anyway, he told me I couldn't have water after electric shock treatment or I'd risk a heart attack. The glimpse of a toilet in the corner of the "operating theater" helped me endure some things. I'd simply imagine crawling to that cool ceramic, lidless pot and lapping the water like a dog, sometimes dunking my whole head in—I was that thirsty! The mind's eye could destroy, but it could also sustain in the strangest ways.

I wonder if they have a toilet where we are going...

The truck stopped and then backed slowly to the direction of outside voices. Seems we moved in reverse forever. At last, a final squeak of the brakes, a crank of the parking brake. Point B, I guess we arrived.

Hushed chatter erupted among us. It struck me as odd how we each sustained wounds, felt sick, hurt miserably, and suffered more than one can envision, but nobody offered comfort in our individual struggles or pain. Fear did that. We learned early on that if we helped each other, displayed compassion, the force repaid us with coldness. Yet, at any sign of variation in our holding tank, we victims conversed in nippy exchanges. Fear did that also. Recognizing our captors meant to kill us threw members of my entourage into a contagious frenzy.

The back of the truck opened. We sounded like a bunch of hounds, sniffing the air, sucking large amounts of atmosphere, even through our hoods. The air felt humid but clean, fresh. Strange, but I felt like a thief for stealing nostrils full of an environment not tainted with undesirable bodily fluids and sour sweat. Relishing an open space struck me with a pang of guilt. The force got to me. Made me believe I was guilty. I must have done something...

Stupid *ajiaco*!

Herded out of the truck, I felt sun on my skin. I enjoyed that, too, until a baton on my back prodded me forward. I experienced relief I could still walk. My mood greatly lifted.

When the ground changed from gravel to a cold, hard surface, the air changed too, from warm and fresh to dank. The sound of our chained feet echoed far, as if our little caravan trudged through a great cavern.

We were shoved into a tightened space and then told to sit and remove our hoods. At first, we called this the processing room, but later we referred to it as the café.

Pus oozed from my eyes, but at least I could open my lids enough to see. I counted nine of us, and what a ghastly sight. Swollen faces, bruised and broken bodies, blood—both dried and fresh—turned my stomach that hadn't been filled in who knows how long.

Our group sat inside a large cylindrical room. The inside walls, painted yellow-beige, seemed rather bright and cheery for holding such downtrodden people. In addition, we had light shining from the rudimentarily wired bulbs overhead. The doors, front and back, made of metal, looked like they belonged on a ship, with wheels to turn in order to seal and make watertight compartments. I wondered about the trickling I heard earlier. Perhaps we were on a ship, but I didn't detect the smell of salt or seaweed in the air when we got off the truck.

We began making small talk, in whispers—those of us who could. Most knew English, to my surprise. I experienced relief with that tidbit. I didn't feel quite so alone knowing I had people to chatter with, other than the "they are going to kill us" man. And another thing, a very important thing—we hadn't seen the evidence of another "operating theater." Maybe those days were over.

The door behind me swooshed open. A waft of new air hit us. I caught a glimpse of sunshine beyond the cylindrical room that continued in the same form, akin to a pipeline. I might have seen mountains across a ravine, but my vision failed. I think we were in a drainage tunnel.

A guard selected two prisoners and took them who knows where, sealing the entry again. A moment later, the door at the other end swooshed, also pipeline beyond, but darker and dank, as if burrowed into the side a mountain. Two new prisoners joined us for the first time.

There we sat, hot, uncertain, slightly hopeful, and naked.

One of the newcomers began talking. His name was Lorenzo. Having been there for a while, he shared with us what he knew of "*La Cueva del Agua*," our prison and our new home.

Nine
The Water Cave

"A jail for political deviants?" I said, with my voice so scratchy and hoarse I didn't even recognize it. "I'm not the least bit political," I huffed. "What am I doing here?" Hyperventilation started to get the best of me. I was having a meltdown. "This is such a terrible misunderstanding. I-I need to tell them, to let them know."

Gloria, a naturally beautiful woman, said with a nod, "*Sí,* sure, all of us here, we are all misunderstood, but do they listen? No. I say no, uh? Look at you. Look at me. Look at him and him and her." She managed to point to everybody. "Tell me this; did they actually accuse you of something? What charges did they bring? Nothing but their torture and names—all they want are names—and a place to put their...you know what I am talking about."

My frame crumpled some. I shivered in spite of the humidity. *Jesus, where are you?* "So, you're not political either?" I coped enough to ask.

She snorted. "What do you think?"

"I can't believe I'm in prison." I expelled a shaky breath. "I'm a good wholesome girl, not an insurgent." A rather large sob escaped, sounding more like a gulp or inhalation working against my deteriorated condition.

"Ugh," Gloria said, shaking her black hair, curls falling around her shoulders, the chains around her wrists in motion clanking together. "They beat you to a pulp, broke you. Look at you," she waved her hand, "you don't even have all of your fingernails, such pretty pink nails."

It was true, and I feared to glance at the little rectangular places where the three yanked nails used to fit. Feeling hot and infected, I couldn't look at my fingers. If I did, it would make the wounds feel worse, as if part of my fingers disappeared too. I noticed her nails. Although fading and chipped red, she still had all of them.

"They left nothing untouched, utter violation," Gloria's hand swooped again, "and you are more concerned about a prison, about a cell, about mistaken identity. *Señora*, they stripped you of identity. Now you have none!"

Someone quieted her down.

Lorenzo said, "Look at this place as more of a reformatory. Here, your chances to die are not as great, if you can..." he shrugged "...reform."

"Wait a minute. Aren't I entitled to a representative from the U.S. Embassy or something? I'm a citizen of the United States!"

"Nobody knows you are here..."

"And reform from what...myself?" My fit of coughing closed that discussion.

"Eh," Gloria nudged me amicably, "Do you have someone?"

"What do you mean?" I asked.

"You know, like a husband or lover, friend, parent...you know, anybody missing you?"

"No," I said quietly. "Well..." I chewed on it. "My parents would miss me if they knew I left home. You see, I came to visit my brother...he's a teacher at a language institute in Bogotá. It was impromptu, the trip. Supposed to be a surprise. But it backfired. He...was having girlfriend trouble...er...trouble with her estranged husband, anyway. Spencer, my brother, made sure I was booked on a flight the very next morning; only he never showed up to take me to the airport." I swallowed hard. At least the swelling had diminished. "I'm so thirsty," I rasped, "Anyway, I spent all afternoon trying to locate him, found his house broken into, messed up, and that night, from outside of my hotel, a nice place to stay, mind you, I was abducted."

"And you do not think this has something to do with your brother? Perhaps, Spencer is involved in subversive political activity," Gloria suggested, "a rebel."

"No way. Absolutely not. Spencer is girl crazy, not political, and certainly not a rebel."

"But his house…"

"Broken into, by a jealous husband of the woman he's living with but shouldn't be living with."

Stillness permeated the space.

"Huh," Gloria said.

"What?"

"So you have nobody who misses you. How sad," Gloria pouted.

I had never thought of it. The awareness did make me sad. I didn't get to dwell on my pity party long, though, for the sound of swooshing echoed in the chamber, blasting us with dankness. Our environment changed again.

It only took one minute to pass from blissful sleep in an upper crusty hotel to the dungeon of doom, one minute to pass from the dungeon of doom to the permanency of imprisonment, one minute to pass from Sylvia Abbott to an emptying shell. One hell to the next equaled one minute each.

A number of guards hustled us to our feet, urging our group to move. I suppose the time allotted to us to act social made us more sympathetic than before, gave us a new dose of humanity, for we attempted to carry the stranded few who couldn't budge. The guards told us to leave them. We never saw those two again.

We were also instructed to leave our hoods behind. I had difficulty coming to grips with that. I think the hood, a small potato sack smelling of burlap, had become my pacifier. Eye infections aside—almost all of us had them—sometimes I liked the hood. Sometimes my worst imagination (hood on) proved better than reality (hood off).

The tunnel ended at a point and we stood in more of a cavern. Water trickled down the walls and drained down small trenches. Lorenzo had told us the pipeline used for drainage from various tributaries to a main river was an old one, retired from its former function, but it made a perfect secret holding tank for political dissidents. Even I thought so. I just didn't belong there.

On both sides of the cavern, rows of small circular doors with wheels, akin to the doors in the processing room, lined the rock walls. The doors had bold black numbers painted on them, but random numbers, not sequential. One by one, the guards motioned for each prisoner to crawl inside. I don't know why, claustrophobia maybe, perhaps after the small taste of civility in the processing room I couldn't muster climbing into that small, dark pod numbered 254. I hesitated, glancing inside. Nothing more than a tube slightly bigger than the average human body, it looked like a sarcophagus to me. Not to mention it had no light source.

A guard prodded me forward but I balked. Then shoving took place. In spite of my miserable physicality, I spread my limbs against the edges of the opening much like a cat against its carrier when you have to transport it to a veterinarian. I felt the rubber blows against my back from the guards' batons, but I wouldn't budge. Next thing I knew, they dragged me away. I had won! Happiness graced me for a second. Then my elation came crashing down when I was led into an operating theater.

My torturer looked bored, in other words, eager to get some business. I had lost. I lost the battle very badly.

In the final lexis of the torturer on duty at that hour, he said, "Maybe we teach you to embrace your new home, uh?"

Indeed, I welcomed it then, cell 254. Although I couldn't scoot into the long, narrow tube, without assistance, that is. Once in, and the door sealed, I forgot about my claustrophobia. Qualms like that wane next to fears that actually inflict pain. I don't know what had come over me, but it wouldn't happen again in terms of dreading confinement in closed, tight spots.

In a strange way, over a little time, the pitch-blackness of my new cell soothed. It was a private space, all my own. I raised my hands to God with what little strength I could muster, thanking him for room to wiggle. However, when my hands stopped within inches of my face, blocked, I broke out in hysterical laughter. The kind of laugh that turns silent, deep, maddened, desperate, until I wept from my grimy eyes.

Finally, I mouthed the words but no sound came out, "*Help, help, help, help.*" I made a plea to my Heavenly

Father, "Don't forsake me. Don't—*please*—don't forsake me..." I sniffed through a congested, bloody nose, and had the foul taste of metal in my mouth. "Oh, you have.... you've abandoned me..."

By day the Lord directs his love, at night his song is with me, a prayer to the God of my life.

I snorted, trying to wipe the oozing moisture from my nose and eyes, as I recalled the scripture that had just popped into my head.

Psalm 42:8. It helps when your dad was a pastor. The requisite for Spencer and me, in order to grow up and abide under his roof peacefully, was Bible memorization.

"Well, this is my night, a whole season of it, twenty-four, seven." *Jesus, I need to know you're still there... please.*

Then a slew of songs rushed my head, filling it with *Emmanuel* this and *Emmanuel* that. Taught the meaning of the word when growing up in church, I pondered the gist of the verses, *God with us.*

"Okay," I whispered in the dark. "Okay."

Apparently, one of the prisoners heard me sing. I didn't think I sang that loud, but his voice started small and then amplified. Others caught on, and before long, the timeless hymn, *Ave Maria,* boomed from our cells. I didn't know any of the words other than "Ave Maria," but I could hum like the dickens. We had ourselves a nice little concert.

Then I heard, "*Silencio! Silencio!*" and excessive pounding on the doors of our tubes rattled our bones. I suppose this was for good measure. Extra threats did wonders.

We quieted, all but the one who started it, the prisoner in the cell next to mine. I heard his door open and the commotion of his body yanked from the tube. Moments later, his screams from The Water Cave's operating theater, our new torture chamber, echoed down the pipeline. At that volume, they ought to hear him all the way to Alaska.

In the midst of this chaos, a familiar notion showed up in my head. Like a flag, it waved, "Hello, look at me, I'm still here and available." Why didn't I consider it before? This is when I formally rediscovered that age-old conquering mechanism.

Prayer.

Nobody would know I'd use it. They could tell me to shut my mouth, but they couldn't shut my mind. They tried to purge my psyche in order to reform it through these, their offenses against humanity, crushing my spirit in the process, yet something lingered. A residual trace of my former life of faith percolated beneath the frail, scarred lining of my being. It wasn't much, but something to build on. I'd start there.

Ten
So Many Ironies

I came down with pneumonia. It was not enough that I had an infection in my eyes, my fingers, my bladder, gashes in the skin, and deepened bruises, bacteria *had* to spread and infect my lungs, too. I had never felt as disintegrated as at that point. I'm not even sure how long I had resided at the prison when this happened, maybe two weeks. Anyway, the pain increased so much I beaded in sweat all over my body, because it took such effort to sip breaths under the duress of hurtful, wet coughing fits.

The decision came, by whom I don't know, to send me to "the infirmary." I had no idea one existed at the prison. Honestly, I didn't think a single soul would care about my new illness, but I rested in a snug cot after guards carried me in on a small stretcher and transferred me to the thing I possessed that actually resembled a bed.

It was a makeshift room, the infirmary, divided by clapboard. Six beds lined the wall, mine among them. The doctor even wore a white coat. The strangest thing, Dr. Gallegos treated me with kindness. He exhibited a gentle and caring demeanor. I couldn't get over it. I thought, surely he's going to start slapping me or something, in the next moment. That notion alone kept apprehension clutched in me. Fear of the authority and of the authority's tools had carved a permanent, controlling mark. I even jumped when the doctor pulled out his stethoscope. I know he noticed, yet he pretended not to. He went about his business in treating people, me since I was the only one present at the time, with helpful professionalism. He gave me drugs.

I felt better.

I slept. Can you imagine after sleep deprivation, how that felt?

Oh, and during this spell, remembrances of Jesus came to the forefront, barging into my consciousness but I wanted to shut him out. Torture made me question how a loving savior could allow this to happen. I was a good person, faithful. I had done my daily devotions, gone to church, prayed. I knew the Bible front to back. My entire life was dedicated to him.

There were moments during interrogation where I had wanted to depart from the earth and join the saints in heaven. Now... I struggled. I struggled with the faith I always thought I had. Having nothing else to do but lay in this cot, I felt somewhat removed from my spiritual convictions, my roots yanked.

Out of habit, forced will, I don't know what, I started to contemplate scripture, more of it. I began recalling verses I had memorized as a youngster. Then I'd stop to think, *what's happened to me is unfair*!

The scriptures would return. I'd dwell on them, only to interrupt with my outbursts.

Unfair!

Then, a variety of artists' renditions of Jesus came to my mind. I saw the Lord struck, ridiculed, maltreated, his back shredded by repeated lashes—this almost forced me to come to terms with injustice, and I didn't like it one bit. I didn't want to come to terms. Not fair!

I blamelessly took on the sins of the world. I took on your *sins. That wasn't fair...*

I told the voice to shut up. It did and I immediately regretted it. I missed it already.

Whatever the doctor gave me ran its full course throughout my body. A fuzzy feeling had come over my head, clouded my mind, and my skin tingled, ears buzzed.

God was supposed to be in control. So where was he? Why has he allowed me to suffer like this? I gritted my teeth against the silence.

A tear slid down my cheek. It might have been hard to detect because of the puffiness and excessive watering of my eyes, but I somehow identified that lone tear. I didn't wipe it, but fell into a semi-hallucinogenic world.

There, I saw Jesus again. He stepped out of a painting, chuckling. As if he possessed a fun little secret he couldn't wait to share, he giggled with a childlike manner. He lifted the hem of his robe a little. It made me curious. I glanced down at his feet, and he wore shiny, black military issued boots. I daresay, combat boots. Like Puma's, the ones I vomited on. Perplexed, my eyes drifted back to the Redeemer's face. However, I didn't glance upon the face of Jesus, but of Puma. Jesus' face had changed to Puma! And he still wore the white robe. Then the visage changed back. At that point, Jesus had a load in his arms, a bundle of something. I moved closer to peek. Again, there was Puma, curled up, a man-sized baby, sleeping in the arms of Jesus. Puma awoke. He smiled. In fact, they both smiled the same type of beam. Their eyes harbored no malice, no heat. I saw compassion, tranquility.

"Jesus, what...?" I shook my head that felt heavy against the cot's mattress, like a brick of mud.

Too confused and upset to speak, Puma did in my stead. The same time I heard his voice, I opened my eyes, which brought me fully back to the prison hospital, the recovery room, and I found Puma standing over my cot.

I clamped my eyes again and began praying out of habit. That's all I could muster. The action came from desperation. Puma terrified me.

A scripture popped in my head, one I'd heard in a sermon shortly before I came to Colombia, and I repeated it as if it were a crazed mantra, *"But I tell you: Love your enemies and pray for those who persecute you, that you may be sons of your Father in heaven. He causes his sun to rise on the evil and the good, and send rain on the righteous and the unrighteous. Matthew 5:44-45."* It was at the word Matthew that I realized I whispered aloud, in a frantic state. I sounded like an insane woman.

I started to shake. The cot quivered, the metal joints squeaking under my trembling frame. I wasn't having a seizure. Seeing Puma sent me reeling with raw emotion. Reality bit.

So! Jesus was on his side, even in my hallucinations.

Your side, too.

This time, I choked back tears. It's finally happened. Psychosis. It's gotten the better of me.

Puma stretched out his hand.

No, no—don't touch me, don't touch...

He hesitated and then timidly retrieved his hand, letting it fall back to his side. Puma backed away slowly, until he disappeared behind a clapboard sectioning. His footsteps quiet, I still detected the sound of his boots until I knew for sure he had left the vicinity. Then I really shook. I thought I'd bounce right out of the cot.

Dr. Gallegos entered from the other side a moment later. "Now, now, what is this? Calm, my child..."

My child?

Seriously?

He stuck a needle in my arm, said it would help me sleep.

Before I nodded off, two guards brought in another prisoner who had just endured torture to the point of urgent care, truly broken. Kind Dr. Gallegos received instructions to nurture the new patient back to health in order for that prisoner to endure more sessions in their *real* operating room. He didn't survive his visit to the infirmary, but left this earth only a few minutes after he arrived.

This is my present and this is my future. I'm supposed to love the one who broke me.

My Father...

Seriously?

Eleven
The Stupid Things Prisoners Do

Overall, our treatment improved at The Water Cave. We still had to endure daily visits to the theater, but it was nothing compared to what we had undergone before.

Once a day, we received a ration of food. At first, they gave us a small plate of beans. Well, mostly beans. We each had the challenge of eating this in the tube, our cell in which we couldn't sit up. In addition, we had to pick out the beans from the worms. Because the drainage tube turned human storage tank had no light, I figured out how to do this by texture. Worms wiggled; beans didn't. If you happened to accidently pop a wiggler in your mouth, worms squirted; the beans were always hard and dry. Spitting proved common practice. In fact, I'd hate the thought of actually having light. I'm sure the walls of my cylindrical crypt left a bit to behold, probably along the lines of an abstract painting. Maybe even a decent one. Something the likes of Picasso might have envied.

Dysentery seemed to be parting for good for me as I grew accustomed to foreign bacteria, and with the fact that our theater sessions continuously lessened. My body was healing. I felt cleaner. Even the lice outbreak came under control when we received a community shower. They ordered us into a little group circle and hosed us down and then treated us repeatedly with lice pesticide in the form of shampoo. After each treatment, we had to rub petroleum jelly on our scalp, eyebrows and eyelashes. I suppose the authority held greater concern regarding the lice outbreak because it had the potential to affect each of them also.

When we prisoners started taking our worm-free meal of beans *and* rice in the original processing room, we inwardly rejoiced. This is when we started calling it our café.

During our visits to the café, the authority allowed us to converse freely. It lightened the mood a bit by feigning dining experiences in high-end restaurants. A regular stage play, we each acted out our favorite make-believe meal. Mine often changed, from steak and lobster, baked potato and chocolate cake, to a take-n-bake pizza and chocolate chip cookies. Movies and popcorn ensued in my performance, while several of the others enjoyed staying out late salsa dancing, or hanging out with friends at a coffee shop, so sometimes, our café changed sets.

I grew attached to Gloria from Medellín. We had very different personalities. She was brazen and loved to talk, and wanted to speak exclusively in English. Although I would have liked to learn more Spanish than I picked up from listening to those around me, namely the guards and other prison officials, she overpowered me in the personality department. So, I enjoyed listening to her, watching her smack her lips and say, "Mm, that was succulent, so divine," as she described her entrée complemented with a glass of Chianti, since she favored anything Italian, from fashion to food and everything in between. Gloria could work as a comedian or actor if she wanted, but she felt content in what she called "the glamour arts."

When I mentioned we could converse freely, I meant anything superficial, small talk. If someone broke into something of the political nature, guards rushed in on that criminal and proceeded to carry that person, or those persons, away to you-know-where. That's when it became clear they monitored everything we said or did, so we sat there and scanned the cracks in the walls of the bare room for an embedded listening device. Dull in our wits, we never expected they'd fix a tap behind the only thing in the café, a circa 1970s framed print of Bogotá. Such an obvious place, we didn't think to look there, until one day Gloria did the honors of actually standing and traipsing over to peek under the frame. She did so without repercussion.

Before we gained knowledge in the particulars of speech, that is, the art of subject-constricted conversation, I did learn a few tidbits about some of the prisoners. For instance, Gloria used to be involved with a guerrilla group turned political party, M-19. But, "no more," she says. She's content to perfect people's makeup and hair, clothes—a regular reformed fashionista. When I asked how she got involved, she said a boy did it...lured her in with his buttery eyes and long lashes, promising a future together.

"Of course, it is always about a boy, uh? Ah, men," Gloria sighed, sinking back against the wall with a playful grin, probably conjuring up some image of one of her former lovers. "You cannot live without them, you cannot live without them."

I chuckled. "I think it's 'you can't live *with* them, you can't live *without* them.'"

"No, I was right the first time," she pointed out.

She made me laugh. I couldn't relate to her on that account, but Gloria helped pass the time by transforming monotony into amusement. I depended on her for that, because staying locked up alone in the tube had its ways of taxing the spirit. It made me eager for the time at the café, eating our high-class meals, sipping Colombian coffee my fellow inmates all insisted proved the best in the world, while elevator music played softly in the background. Ah, the pleasantries proved so pleasant, so relaxed and superficial, so different from the dark, empty shell, my tube, with only room enough to stuff my body.

Yet, even in there, cell 254, I had my diversions. We all did. For instance, in order to avoid those nasty bedsores from lying in one position for too long, I would try to turn. Tricky to perform, but I managed to do a complete circle in about a minute by inching my way around. I created a race. It got my adrenaline going. It also made a lot of noise, but I worked on that test, too—how to turn as fast as you can without a sound. Difficult...*muy, muy difícil*, but it passed the time.

Another thing. I enjoyed decorating my cell. Of course, I couldn't move much in the pinched space. However, in the dark, space has no dimension, so I decorated it in my mind's eye, as if a living room in a waterfront condominium. First, I selected a traditional décor, then colonial, modern and French provincial. Once, I even designed a log cabin, chalet style, or do they call it A-frame?, full of rugged features, such as a chandelier made of antlers. Not usually my cup of tea, but in prison you do the oddest things. Out of all, minimalism turned out as my favored interior design. Go figure.

I found it fun to pretend I laid in a space capsule about to launch and I was an all-important astronaut, a sexy one who had it all going for her. Kind of like Gloria.

And my all-time favorite stupid thing to do: recite nursery rhymes. The best one of all, hands down, was the tongue tying Thomas a Tattamus. Of course, in it I tried to count all the *T*s...

My answer came out wrong every time. I'm not a numbers person.

Now, back to the celebrated café.

We political prisoners who did not have permission to speak of our accounts of torture or officials in the prison, discovered even that changed after a while. I'm not sure why. Perhaps, those listening saw it as part of our reformation to accept what happened to us, rather than deny or question the evidence of the accounts, as they originally wanted us to do, and grant us the liberty of having our little fun with it.

At first we began with code numbers in referring to methods of torture. For instance, if a technique proved especially bad, it deserved a ten, the others fit in underneath ten and over one. Wait—yeah, that's right. One to ten described the level of dislike associated with the method, and we disliked them all. The numbers became the titles. Little by little, we began addressing the methods by their real references.

While I'm sure a zillion others exist—evil is present after all, and man has had centuries to come up with this stuff—here is a compiled list of what we personally endured since our capture:

La Picana: This was the most utilized, because it left little to no traces of its purpose. Also called Carolina, or Rita, and sometimes Duke (don't ask). Electric shock via cattle prod, meant to tenderize you like a steak—oh, and spew names! I still think of Eduardo Corrochio and cringe with remorse. Never would I have thought...

La Parilla: The grill. Some called this The Rack. You're tied to the metal frame of a bed where you receive electric shock treatments. Of course, all of this is much worse if they douse you with water, which leads me to one I especially hate...

El Submarino: I heard this described in various forms at the café. With me, they tied a hood over my head and plunged it in water, or, tilted me back and then they poured water over my face. Together, hood and water, they made a perfect union that gave the sensation of suffocating, drowning. Once I got this treatment strapped tightly to a board and plunged backwards into a tub. Couldn't move, couldn't breathe. They sometimes did this to the point of passing out. I fear water, so it doubly stunk.

Water cure: Some called this snorkeling. Nose is pinched, mouth wedged open and stuffed with a funnel. Forced to guzzle water often mixed with urine to the point of severe stomach distention; beating sometimes quickens the response of vomiting. After which point they repeat the exercise.

Waterboarding: Before my capture, I had heard of this in my own country, but I think the technique varies. Though one prisoner here spoke of it, the rest of us didn't experience this. I have to give voice to that one person. In his words, it's a maddening drip, drip, drip, drip without ceasing, is how he put it. "Drip, drip, drip, drip." Literally, he wouldn't stop. I think every single one of us blinked every time he said, "drip," sensing his psychosis. We had to snap him out of his trance before he sucked us in with him.

Pau de arara: I believe this is a Portuguese term, according to Lorenzo anyway. A pole over the arms and behind the knees with wrists and ankles tied together. The whole thing suspended, it appears like a parrot's perch. This gave me headaches like you wouldn't believe, and I'm not prone to headaches, not to mention muscle and joint pain.

Garrote: They actually had a specially designed chair for this with a wooden pole up the spine. It looked medieval. Can you imagine working as the carpenter on such a thing? Anyway, you sat in the chair while they strapped your neck to the pole in a band attached (like a collar). Your interrogator turned a rod fixed at the back of the collar, which tightened the band at each crank, leading you to the point of strangulation.

Bastinado, or *foot whipping*: The bottoms of your feet are beat extensively with a rubber hose. Extremely painful and takes a long time to heal. This proved popular also, because it's quite effective yet leaves little in the way of residual physical marks.

Strappado: Hands tied behind your back, they hang you up by a rope. This leads to arm dislocation. Sometimes they add a weight to the bottom to increase the pain and speed up the process. Although I've hung, tethered by arms over the head, I didn't have to experience this particular version as another prisoner did.

Teeth pulling: Self-explanatory. As I glanced at a prisoner, an elderly man named Pablo, thankfulness filled me with the fact that I still have all of mine.

Denailing: Also self-explanatory, however, I will add "excruciating." I'm missing three. After infections and all, they are healing. Dr. Gallegos cleaned them out, not pain-free, mind you. I can look at them now, all my fingers.

They're strange, the ones without the nails. The kind doctor told me they would grow back, but it would take time. He mentioned this fact as if I'd live long enough to witness the nail rebirth. Well, he felt all but one would return anyway. He said the matrix of one fingernail bed looked too badly damaged.

There exists a host of other violations, such as cutting, bruising and beating, etc., and then we have the psychological forms of torture, such as sleep deprivation, starvation, various forms of humility, such as name-calling, kowtowing, assuming positions meant to bring embarrassment, sexual molestation, groping, and rape. You'd think the rape and such would fall under the physical abuses category, but easily, we all felt it injured our self-worth and psyches more than anything, especially among us females. It proved the ultimate violation, above all, when conducted with a joking, or mocking air, as opposed to purely animalistic aggressiveness.

Then we have the instruments of torture, some of what I mentioned above prove a part of this list, but a few interrogators used nicknames for things such as pliers, rods, scissors, hammer, chisel, drills, screwdrivers, clamps—they almost always had feminine names, or titles suggesting comfort and coziness. Again, with the ironies, we have *Mamacita, Linda, Hada Madrina* (fairy godmother), etc. The worst was *La Princesa*, in which one interrogator, who was especially fond of thespian roles, began proclaiming, *"La princesa está triste..."* He'd pensively turn the gadget in his palm. "The princess is sad, uh? But you, I think, will make her very, very happy." He'd smirk and then apply *La Princesa*, indeed making her very, very happy.

When we, the prisoners, began discussing this more freely, no guards came to haul us away. Still.

Expanding our rediscovered egos a bit, we continued to exchange notes, progressing to the *handlers* of the methods: take a bow, our torturers.

Twelve
Episode of the Blue Sweater

For whatever reason, the regular hour for our meal in the café came and went without our discharge to go and eat. In prison life, a perplexing fixation took place. An internal clock somehow latched itself inside my bosom, telling me of things such as this little schedule of ours that the authority averted. I suppose it's the extreme monotony tantalizing us with the one thing we all grew to enjoy, our hour in that café.

I had been praying for my enemies, again, a recent regular practice, when I started to feel more antsy than usual. When I heard others banging against their cell doors and shouting, I understood what that meant. We wouldn't shuffle to our watering hole, sit upright, talk, and eat—no café today. I wondered why we deserved this punishment. But that was a stupid thing to ponder. If I allowed myself, I'd spend eternity musing about punishment as a whole and search for answers I'd never receive, because nothing made sense. In that manner, eternity would just turn into another extension of hell.

Not getting to go to the café also meant I wouldn't get to use the one bathroom the authority allowed us once a day. After training to *hold it* for unreasonable lengths, I'd have to resort to *going* within my little space capsule again.

The prisoners revolted with a rumpus. Well, it was a dull rumpus, because really, how much noise can you make with bare hands and feet extended from physically weak bodies and voices crusty from malnutrition and prolonged dehydration, forced in positions that left little room for maneuvering? On the plus side, I had little to no concern for my time of the month. I don't know if it was the poor nourishment or the stress, but that seemed to dry up and disappear along with everything else.

Our rebellion brought the guards rapping on our cells, telling us to shut up, but after a while, when the commotion didn't cease, they began letting us out, one by one. There we all stood, staring at each other with blank expressions, wondering whom they would drag to the theater first, but they didn't drag anybody. We received no browbeating, and no violent repercussions. They allowed us to stand there while they explained that the person who prepared our food hadn't shown up. As a result, we didn't get to go to the café for fear we'd revolt there. However, it made no difference where the upheaval happened. With us having been reduced to nothing but frail objects, they didn't have much with which to contend. Once they realized that, they behaved more amicably.

My legs trembled from standing. About to slide down to squat on the floor, I stopped when I noticed a female guard. Something struck me as odd about her appearance. I'd seen her before—it wasn't that she was unknown to me—but it was what she wore. It looked familiar. The guard leaned against the wall not that far away. I shuffled over to her, inch by inch. My eyes didn't deceive me. She wore my blue sweater, the one my mom had given me! An embroidery nut, my mom embroidered all three of my initials on it. I hated the sweater because of that. I mean, who wants to walk around with S.P.A. on it? Really, why didn't my mother consider this when she selected Patricia as my middle name? Didn't she put the letters together first, try them out? Anyway, it's probably not a big deal, but when teased as a kid because of it, things have a way of exacerbating your emotive outlook. Having explained all that, I still kept the sweater because it was one of my warmest.

But now this female guard wore it. You can't imagine how it felt to see something from my luggage covering her torso without my permission, while I'm naked and have been for such a long time I forgot what fabric felt like, aside from the stiffness of the authority's uniforms around here. What other things of mine did she have? Where was my stuff?

I lunged at the guard. Well, more like I threw myself on her in the form of a tripped-up fall, but the feeling was all there. I tried to rip that sweater off her. She swiped back, and we got into this brawl. Lord, I always hated things like catfights, but there I was, reacting with feline ferocity. I'd tear that sweater off one thread at a time if I had to!

They bludgeoned me. I didn't care. I wanted my sweater. The amount of strength I exuded at that moment proved startling. It came from anger. Rage stuffed deep inside, in some unknown pocket, suppressed anger, lashed out with all its might. Foreign to me, this fury, I couldn't control it and they couldn't control me.

The next thing I knew, sections of the pipeline's ceiling rushed by at dizzying speed. Then I heard my fellow prisoners shouting my name.

"Sylvia!" bounced off the walls and echoed down the corridor.

I wondered at that second how long my prisoner friends had urged me to stop. I hadn't heard anything before that point, except the erratic and heavy thumping of my heart pounding on my eardrums in deafening measure.

Dumped in the theater in crumpled form, I curled up into a ball and shook from crying so deep it came out silent. I don't know how long I did this, but after a stretch, when the crying lessened, I detected the room had another occupant. Of course it did—the torturer for that hour. Then curiosity struck me as to why the occupant didn't do his job.

Uncurling, I peeked.

Puma stood with his back turned to me. Leaning on the long workbench, his hands splayed, holding his weight, he rocked slightly.

I dreaded the sight of him. He was my first time, the one who propelled me into this unforgiving hell, and he hated me—every fiber convinced me of that. On a number of occasions, he had loosed on me the same kind of fury I'd unleashed on that female guard wearing my ugly-warm blue sweater.

Although I knew he had come to The Water Cave, I hadn't seen him during any of my sessions. The others talked about Puma, of course, for he made the top of their lists as their favorite. His shift never corresponded with my trips to the theater, I guess, to my good fortune. In the prison's infirmary, while recovering from pneumonia (among a host of other things), I saw him then. That was the only time, but it proved more than enough. I thought he reached out to strangle me, but he left the room in some form of distraction. I remember listening keenly to his boots against the hard floor, until I couldn't hear his footsteps anymore.

He didn't move. I waited. Still, he didn't budge. The anxiety of watching him in this stealth mode overwhelmed me.

Would I die by his hand tonight...today...whatever time it was? I could see it now, clearly. I began to understand how the system worked. Death over my little blue sweater, a gift from my mom, embroidered with S.P.A., proved my perfect demise, something with which to seal my gift of capture—a bow of absurdity.

It began with Puma, why not come full circle and end it with Puma? At the end, everybody would find happiness. They would get rid of me, Puma could salsa on my unmarked grave, and I would go to Jesus and ask him about this rude interruption in my life. Yes, the Big Why. I figured if I made it that far, to the pearly gates, that is, I ought to be granted the chance to ask.

Struggling to my hands and knees, I crawled to the rack, collapsing against the sharp, cutting metal frame. The springs against my back gave when I pulled myself on, squeaking with every bouncy wave, as if saying "Sucker, sucker, sucker..."

Puma tilted his head then. He turned slightly, eyeing me with suspicion.

I shifted to stare at the ceiling, awaiting the purge through the ambiance of electrified burning and the sense of melting organs. It seemed moments went by when he ambled to *La Parilla*. I supposed I should have tied myself to the frame, too, but that's a bit difficult to do.

Waiting, I waited. And waited...

Dropping my head to the side, I dared glance at him only to say, "It's my sweater." I felt the need to declare my side of the story before I perished.

Resuming my position, I counted the cracks in the ceiling.

I tallied 43 cracks when I realized Puma was there at my side. He stroked my cheek.

Oh dear, so that's how he wants it...

Not Puma's nature, not like Frick, anyway, it caught me off guard. I closed my eyes and tried to steady my breathing.

The funny thing is, it didn't feel creepy, his touch. Gentle, almost tender, I thought, this is a new tactic for him: Make her melt with my sudden compassion, weaken, expecting softness, and then, wham! Surprise her with a new measure of my magnificent brutality.

A sob escaped my throat. When I built enough courage to glance at him, he retracted a little, only to touch not only my cheek, but my temple and the crown of my head, too. His stroking still mild, his green-gold eyes even reflected soft pools rather than the inferno I had come to know.

I didn't understand what compelled this outburst, but I blubbered, "I don't know anything about politics..." and then I inhaled a series of gasps, I suppose trying to cry at such a deep, dark level in which my chest constricted and my body tried to remember how to function. To weep, to laugh—I almost forgot how to do those basic things. My mind, wracked with such confusion, emptied of everything and seemed to shut down. But I remember him saying one thing.

"I know."

Puma picked me up, cradled me as I'd seen Jesus cradle him during my drug-induced hallucinations at the clinic. We drifted to a dark corner of the room where we sank in a chair, my crumpled body held against him like a baby. He made me swallow some pills. I don't remember much else before the guards came to take me back to my space capsule.

Thirteen
Disorientation

I saw my brother.

He stood in the middle of a field.

Spencer smiled. I don't know how I got there, or why I stood at the edge of that field, but there I waited for him. Perplexed, I tried to return the smile, but realized how dreadful I must look. Did I even wear clothes? I glanced down, yes, a light blue denim dress. I don't understand where it came from, but there it was, and I felt relieved. Lifting my head, I waved to him. He appeared unsure, but, slowly, he waved back.

I motioned for him. He didn't budge. With more enthusiasm, I persuaded him to come to me, but Spencer wouldn't move. He just stood there, pushing his eyeglasses back into place. Muttering under my breath, I started into the field, pressing long grass down with each step. Mesmerized by the sway of the wispy stalks in the wind, I didn't notice Spencer signaling me away. The closer I got, the more I witnessed sweat stains on his shirt. In fact, wetness dripped from him. He made those familiar nervous gestures I always found annoying. Spencer bordered on frantic. I stopped and so did the sound of the breeze brushing strands of the long green grass, the only sound of my awareness.

Puzzled, I tilted my head. I could feel my own brow furrow. It appeared as if he stared past me. The expression he wore gave me chills.

Like honey on a cold day, I turned to see what Spencer saw. A mountain lion, sleek, stealthy, powerful, slinked toward me. The animal's intentions clear, I gasped. Looking at my brother again to tell him to run, I saw a different man standing there. No... it was Spencer but a different version of him. His light blue denim shirt ripped half off, the rest of his body was bare. Bloodstains marked his chest, his glasses missing.

Oh Spencer, I thought, but couldn't speak.

Bared arms reached for him. Arms I hadn't noticed before. They rose from the earth, and that's when I saw a cluster of corpses, dark-stained, nude, broken, swollen, fractured, disfigured, surrounding him. In fact, he stood in the middle. The bodies reached for him, as if actors from some well-done, realistic zombie movie, pulling him down into the earth with them. I screamed into my hands, but no actual sound reverberated in the tube in which I hallucinated.

Spencer gazed at me one last time with his hand out, gesturing for me to stay, to be still. Calmness overtook him, as did the arms. He smiled at me sweetly then, the way I remember him when we were at our best. My big brother who I loved with all my heart, the closest friend I ever had.

While growing up, he always gave me the best half of everything, the bigger slice of pie and the extra cherry from his ice cream sundae. While our religious parents were set against it, Spencer snuck me out, taking me trick-

or-treating, stuffing our pillowcases full of candy at Halloween every year until I turned twelve. He woke me up at four in the morning to go through Christmas stockings, where he always had an extra special gift just for me. He kept me out of trouble, helped me with my homework and protected me (as best he could) from the school's Twinkie bullies. He pulled my toes, making them pop and crack. I hated that, but it made me laugh so bad I even peed in my pants once. He never let me forget it.

Spencer and his playful jokes, Spencer and his nose-bridge pinching, his arm smacks and big bear hugs, his sarcasm, the whininess to his voice when he got upset, his sensitivity when I hurt his feelings, Spencer at his best and worst...

Spencer disappearing...

I mouthed the word, *NO*. Trembling, I shook my head, but nothing could bring him back.

Nothing remained but an empty field and the return of the wind sweeping the grass as if untouched.

Then I remembered the mountain lion, but didn't much care at that moment. I turned to look at it more out of curiosity than dread, for numbness trounced me before the animal did. Surprised to see Puma, the man, standing where the lion had been, I watched him, void of feeling.

His head was bowed. When he brought it up to meet my line of sight, our eyes locked. We stared at each other. Never able to detect what he thought, or how he'd behave, he surprised me again by walking away into a nearby thicket. I watched his back, the shine of his black hair under the sun. Through the trees, I caught a glimpse of white. I pressed in for a closer look and saw Jesus. *My* Jesus walked with Puma through the jungle path. I decided to follow, but they moved ahead so quickly I couldn't keep up. Finally, I sank to the ground.

The sun descended rapidly. I sat in darkness, but I heard a voice, "Pray for him."

Pray for who—Spencer?

My question met silence.

Oh, I knew it, I knew it, I sobbed, rocking in a fetal position, the chill of the night air poisoning my skin. My brother was dead.

"Pray for him."

Who? I screamed.

I shrieked a second time—because I knew. I knew what the Lord was asking of me and I didn't think I could do it, not now. Not now when I knew Spencer no longer lived.

Puma had been one of the men at the hotel lounge asking about my brother. It didn't make sense that they'd take him, but neither did it make sense that they'd 'disappear' me too. Spencer was dead! Spencer was dead, and nobody knew where I was. I might as well die too. There is no logic here!

I moaned. That's when Jesus whispered in my ear, but I interrupted him because the fragrance of him proved paradise enough. "Let me...let me stay with you," I said.

I must go.

"Let me go with you," I begged.

I have something yet for you to do...

"Anything, just don't stop loving me. I've forgotten what it's like in your presence." I inhaled deeply and sighed with content.

Pray for him.

"Oh," I whimpered. "I had already forgotten about him."

I have not.

"I know." The dark was so suffocating I could only detect the aura of my Lord, a vague outline of light against the backdrop of gloom. "Puma."

Yes.

When he affirmed it, he uttered that single word with such enthusiasm and compassion I found the real love he had for this man, my torturer. How could it be? The depth of it sent vibrations throughout my body. Kind, placating, comforting vibrations offset anything else at that moment. I sat in his presence after all. How would it fare when I plummeted back to my hell on earth, my tube? I reached out and pressed my hands against the metal wall of my cell. I had never left it.

I tried to talk, but words wouldn't come out. I turned my head back and forth to wake up, only I had never fallen asleep. The pills Puma had given me put me somewhere in between.

Awareness crept back. A chill climbed over my skin. Lying in my cold cell, my lashes beat against the blackness, but it didn't matter how much I did that, try to discern something out of nothing. Light would not materialize when none existed.

Though I didn't exactly agree to the deed, that is, Jesus' personal request, I recited the scripture that came to me while in the hospital... "*But I tell you: Love your enemies and pray for those who persecute you, that you may be sons of your Father in heaven. He causes his sun to rise on the evil and the good, and send rain on the righteous and the unrighteous.*"

Spencer's face kept inching into my mind's eye, but I pushed it down with the repetition of the scripture. I was afraid if I stopped and my brother came full into view, taking over, I'd never be able to pray again, and certainly not for my perpetrator.

"Help me, Lord," I prayed. "Help me to pray for Puma, because I don't want to," I sobbed. "I hate him, I hate him, I hate him, I hate him."

Love.

No!

Love—

No!

Love—

Stop.

Love—

I can't.

You can. Love—

The banshee Sylvia screamed again, enraged.

There was a pause. "Jesus...?"

Silence filled the tube.

I panicked. "Don't leave me."

Love.

"I'll try."

"That's all that I ask," he replied. "I never said it would be easy, but I'll be with you. Lean on me. I've missed you."

I've missed you, too. I wept while warmth covered me in an unseen blanket.

Fourteen
The Informant

I had demanded to see a representative from the U.S. Embassy, even though Lorenzo had warned me not to. I didn't, or maybe couldn't, listen to him. In fact, I asked specifically for Chuck Goren. Mr. Goren easily became my middle name (I desired a new one anyway). Taught a very hard lesson, I persisted, and again against Lorenzo's stern counsel.

We'd sit in the café and he'd say, "No, Sylvia, behave wisely. Then you might survive. Consider this. Would you not say a chance at life is worth it?"

"But I'm entitled, I'm a US citizen. And what kind of life is this anyway, spent in a prison deep within a mountain's bowels, where nobody knows where I am?"

"Precisely. You are a U.S. citizen clandestinely abducted and held against her will. How do you think this piece of news will fare for them, the authority, in the end?"

"So, they're in trouble because of me?" I said, in more of a statement than a question.

"Not as long as nobody knows you are here," he answered anyway.

"So it would behoove them to finish me off."

"It would behoove them to end it if they could dispose of your body without a trace. That is not easy, you know, to make a person disappear forever." Lorenzo shrugged.

I shivered.

"Make them think you have reformed. Forget about the injustices you feel. Play them at their own game, but get better at it. Once on the outside, do what you must."

"Lorenzo," I said, shaking my head. "Do you not see they have no benefit in releasing me? If it's as you say I'm a risk to them. I can jeopardize their reputation by bringing public exposure to their dark little secret. If I were they, I'd never release me." I sighed. "It's a losing situation, I'm afraid. Us and them at an impasse, gridlocked." I used my hands, intertwining my fingers.

"Now you know the nature of politics," he flippantly remarked.

"But I'm not political, and this is my life!"

"This is theirs, too." He shifted. "Sylvia, you are a woman of faith, yes?"

I gave him the faintest nod. He nodded, too, but his was more pronounced.

"Stay under the radar," he whispered. "Keep low and undetected. After a while, you never know. They may soften, allow you to slip through the cracks. But if you aggravate them, create scenes, fight," he said with finesse, "you have no hope." After he squeezed my shoulder, he ignored me.

I slumped back against the wall. Subsequent to repercussive treatments conducted by the men at attention at the machine, that is, electric shock treatments, you'd think I'd learn not to ask for anything.

Lorenzo was right. I just didn't understand why he chose to help me with those words of advice. I liked him.

We were friends. But we prisoners all knew the authority had planted Lorenzo there among us as an informant, listening to our innermost conversations, studying our behavior. Apparently, the listening device behind the framed picture wasn't enough. I suppose they had to have someone on the inside to gain our trust, or monitor our hushed dialogue. If I wore his shoes, I'd feel greatly disappointed. None of us ever spoke of anything important. If a revelation came, it wouldn't come from any of us.

One day, the café door leading to the exiting portion of the pipeline swooshed open mid-meal. As if on cue, Lorenzo put down his plate of rice and beans, stood and shuffled out. We never saw him again.

Fifteen
Ups & Downs

Prison life improved to an even larger degree. For one thing, we earned clothing. I'm not sure what we did to deserve the enhancement. I suppose we had taken on a sort of metamorphosis in that we accepted our lot, fell into a routine, their routine. We couldn't fight the system, so we blended in, which is exactly what Lorenzo cautioned us to do.

Good old Lorenzo. I wondered where he was. In his home, perhaps, donning a satiny smoking jacket, watching *fútbol*, making love to his wife of forty-six years, or playing with his grandkids. I tried to imagine his life on the outside. The funny thing about it, I could do so without resentment. I truly hoped he enjoyed himself, because I genuinely liked him. In a strange way, he looked out for me.

It happened at our next mealtime, the clothes. We shuffled our feet along as best you can do while chained, gaining proficiency over time. Had I known that would be the last time we'd wear shackles, in my head I would have drawn out the drama of the transition. As it turned out, we entered the café, the guards removed each cuff and chain, dragging it all away with such clamor I wanted to cup my ears, but I didn't. I forced myself to listen to the clang of iron go away, a moment I had desired ever since they slapped the binds on me. I closed my eyes and breathed in and then out. They were gone. I'd remember the feeling forever.

I studied the marks on my wrists and ankles caused from the cuffs, knowing if I lived long enough to have my own children, I'd have scars to talk about to them, teaching them the important lessons in life. As I rubbed them, I mused on those lessons. One, yield when demoralized by a system; two, pray for your enemies.

Ah, but I could hear the children asking, "Why?" to the first rule, as well as, "Why?" to the second.

Both of which my single answer would have to resound, "I don't know."

"But Mommy, how did you get to that scary place?"

"I don't know."

Then when I had grandchildren, they would begin to ask, to get cut off by their parents as I hear them, my adult children, whisper harshly, "Shh, we don't talk about that around Nana."

If I did find freedom from this place and resumed a normal life, I don't think my existence would ever take the shape of normality again. The Water Cave would draw me back every day, and many moments throughout the day. There wouldn't exist a single morning in which I would not wake up and think of this place, relief rushing through me once I discovered I no longer resided here. Instead, I abided in my own home, with my husband, knitting needles and my favorite chair.

Gloria kept slapping my arm, trying to get my attention.

"What?"

She pointed to the pile of clothes I had missed. How did I not see it? I guess the shackles broken open, lifted, and carried away engulfed me.

"Clothes!" Gloria grabbed my shoulders, as if snapping me out of a trance. Her natural giddiness had a way of affecting me, making me smile, but I hesitated. Any moment I expected the guards to come in, snatch the clothes away (or set them on fire), and slap those chains back on. The same as waving a lollipop in front of a child, taunting him or her, with no intention of actually giving the candy to the youngster who grabbed at it with two eager hands and wide eyes of innocence, it could come down as a cruel joke.

We sorted through the heap of denim…jail duds you could call them. Faded, worn thin, light blue material that struck me as a cheap imitation. I remembered my recent drug-induced hallucination of Spencer, his blue denim shirt, my blue denim dress. Feeling dizzy, I sat down.

"What is the matter?" Gloria inquired.

"Nothing," I waved my hand, dismissing it. "Just not feeling well."

"It is difficult to feel well here. But look, Sylvia," she displayed a dress, holding it up against her hourglass figure. "Ah, I feel like a model." She played with the fabric.

I smiled. "You look like one." I didn't want to mention the recent figments of my delirium, which included this same blue faux denim. A big part of me didn't want to admit my hallucinatory visions, other than the part with Jesus. I relished that much of it. The rest gave me a sinking feeling in the pit of my stomach.

Ah, but they removed our shackles! Now we have clothing. We were more civilized, at least.

"Here, try this one." Gloria tossed me a dress.

I tossed it back as if infected. "I want the overalls," I said, asking her by hand motion to bring me the more official-looking garments.

"Those are for the men," Gloria looked at me quizzically.

"Is that what they said?"

"*Sí.* Take the dress." She tossed it back to me where it fell in my lap. I stared at it as if it carried a bad omen.

I sighed. If I had to pray for my enemies, I suppose I needed something like a prayer shawl to cover my back, at least. Starting with some basic clothing would do.

Slipping the dress over my head, it fell over my emaciated body. Not a bad fit, at all. I was surprised.

"Ah," Gloria beamed, encouraging me to embrace the moment. "Looking good."

"Thanks," I grinned. "You too."

A scrap broke out between two prisoners over a pair of pants, interrupting our self-adoring moment. The rest of us attempted to quiet the pair down. We tried to get the most sensible one to concede in an amicable manner. Fearing the guards would come in, we were troubled they'd punish us by stripping us, again, and taking all the clothing away.

When it finally calmed in the café, we enjoyed a lazy meal, this time a picnic in a park, sunlight basking us with warmth. Children played, conversation lulled, we listened to the birds chirping, dogs in the distance barking. A pleasant reverie, it all folded in on itself, crashing until the screen went blank when the exiting door opened and a guard took a very confused and somewhat hesitant Gloria away.

"I will be back. You will see. We will see each other again." Gloria spoke in a manner of convincing herself.

Famous last words, I thought.

I didn't say goodbye. Goodbye sounded too final. However, she never returned. Day after day, I hoped for news of her, but the guards never spoke to us, never answered questions. In fact, confronting them, sometimes a mere glance, making eye contact, provoked ill treatment. I might have clothing but I was still a dog to them, just a clothed one.

Losing Gloria sent me into a deeper depression. Not only my friend, she proved my crutch in conversation, as well. Her understanding of the English language aided me a great deal. We conversed well. Besides all that, she made me laugh. Gloria had a great love and enthusiasm for life and culture. She managed to bubble positivity in a bubble-less dungeon. Take her away and I stared at the walls or the other faces that looked just like mine, hollow and drawn, and I deteriorated.

It got so bad I kept to myself and stopped trying to communicate with anybody. I lost interest...not in them, in life.

I prayed for Gloria. The only thing that could pull me out of my melancholic overdose was when I thought of her at liberty, hoping the system had freed her. Yes, I prayed for her life, her strong persona not just surviving but also spreading that catching, joyful, innate passion of hers to others as she did to me.

Live long and live well, Gloria!

Once, when I climbed into my tube after a trip to the café, I cried over my friend because I missed her. It amazed me how attached, how close a human can draw to another in a relatively short amount of time under desperate measures.

Daily treatments lessened to about a few times a week. That proved another thing for which I thanked the Lord. Even those sessions seemed to grow milder. Our perpetrators digressed. It seemed they did all they could do with us. Now we subsisted while they moved on to other things.

Then the monotony killed me. I could laugh at my choice of words here, but it's true. Everything so repetitious, boring, with lack of purpose, and significance—I could say it's almost as bad as the treatments. But...no, no, no, nothing is worse than say, *La Parilla*...especially when tagged on after *El Submarino*...and, well, everything, everything else was worse, the whole gamut. So, never mind. That was a stupid thing to say. It surfaced out of boredom.

Another thing swelling out of tedium, a positive item, was prayer. I found my life of spiritual meditation deepening. I had hated Puma. I began by asking God to replace that strong emotion with another, that of love. The Lord wanted me to love my enemies. Puma proved my enemy again and again. I didn't have it in me to do it on my own, so I continued to request help. I needed the heavenly backup. You know, I *still* hated him, but not as much. I figured with time, my emotions would go through a metamorphosis and I'd come out a butterfly for doing my duty. Now, if only I could fly away.

I saw Puma recently, actually. We passed in the pipeline, as we victims journeyed to the café to eat. His head tilted down, a position he seemed especially comfortable in, he glanced up and slowed when he noticed me. The first time we saw each other since my shackles disappeared and the clothing went on. Funny thing, when all of us sulked around in the nude, the authority had seen so much of us and we prisoners of each other that nothing contained interest. Now, with prison garb donning our human frames, those around us peered with a bit of curiosity. Puma was no different. Yet when he did so, something unusual transpired. It was not the eyes dancing up and down the body, filled with odd interest. He didn't do that. He took note of the clothes, as if assessing how they fit, and then he gave me an intent look as if he couldn't see anything else.

The other prisoners had passed me. The rear guard started to propel me along. My eyes glued onto Puma. He shared the same conduct. We didn't stop looking at each other until the guard closed me inside the café, shutting the door on Puma's frozen silhouette in the pipeline.

To this day, I have no idea what happened there between us—but something did. If I could describe it, it would be an exchange of some sort. I more or less just explained how we stopped and stared in the tunnel, but what transpired was much more than that. I just don't...I really don't know *what*, exactly.

Puma held a quiet intensity. He always possessed a quiet intensity, but there was that softness again. It was real, evident. Similar to when he held me in the operating theater, right before he made me swallow the pills. His demeanor differed from before. It caught me off guard. I comprehended that I had hated him because of what he did to me. My abductor, my first interrogator, not only vicious and enraged, he catapulted me into this unending misery. The others, his colleagues, horrible in their own ways, would never compare to Puma, because Puma served as my initial rude disruption for which my life will never recover, never be the same again. I hated him also because I *wanted* to. I wanted to blame him. I *needed* to blame somebody.

However, when he held me in the operating theater, and when we just passed in the tunnel and stopped to swap gazes, it was a little more difficult to feel that magnitude of abhorrence, and I hated *that*! More ironies! I prayed for him because the Lord asked me to. I pled with the Lord to replace the hate with love, yet when he did so, I fought it.

I didn't really want to love Puma but I had to try. My spirit battled flesh. I knew what God wanted me to do. I just found it so hard. It would take more prayer.

Good thing I had time.

Strange to ponder, torture reduces a person to nothing. In many ways, one feels like an empty shell, void of spirit, negating things that make you, you. The fight in you departs at some point. I succumbed easily under my perpetrators' muscle, and here, my Creator of all the earth—that included these monsters, my Almighty God—who is Lord of all and reigns supreme, asks me to do a simple task and I fight him tooth and nail.

Maybe doubt crept in while my body and spirit broke, reduced to nonentity through shame and abuse. Perhaps I questioned God's existence. After all, my perpetrators told me *they* were god. Perchance, I believed it. They could be very convincing.

However, now...now the real God persuades me. Anxieties plague me as well. I see purpose to them. I can comprehend the sorrow, the significance, the task, but I feel so weak, incapable.

Unworthy.

A song popped into my head just now. *Worthy is the Lamb who was slain...*

Ah, Jesus, you went as a lamb to the slaughter for me, for humankind, for...yes, for Puma. I swallowed the lump in my throat when I imagined the ultimate persecution, the ultimate sacrifice. Seems the reminder was coming to me more often these days.

I get it, Lord. I'm *trying* to get it.

For the first time, I slightly bowed my head and whispered over my plate of dry beans and crunchy rice, and asked Jesus to turn something ugly into something beautiful. I gave that situation, my confinement to The Water Cave, to him to do with what he wills. Whatever the outcome, I wanted to dwell in his perfect will, and I asked that he receive glory from it.

Expressing a manner of prayer through memorized scripture, I uttered, "And we know that in all things God works for the good of those who love him, who have been called according to his purpose."

I had to trust Him on this.

The book of Romans kept niggling. "What, then, shall we say in response to this? If God is for us, who can be against us? He who did not spare his own Son, but gave him up for us all—how will he not also, along with him, graciously give us all things? Who will bring any charge against those whom God has chosen? It is God who justifies. Who is he that condemns? Christ Jesus, who died—more than that, who was raised to life—is at the right hand of God and is also interceding for us." I whispered this again.

As I prayed for Puma, per the Lord's request, I realized Jesus was interceding for me.

Through this, through *him*, we were connected, Puma and I.

A puff of air escaped my lungs. I rubbed my face with my hands.

I didn't eat my meal. Instead, I prayed, slouched in the corner of the café, ignored by the others, awestruck by the Word of God and grateful, again, that my parents made me memorize scripture. Who would have thought that I'd need it as I do now? *They* must have. Thank you, Mom and Dad. It was my redeeming feature in that hour.

Later, I'd probably regret not consuming all of my two scoops of food. However, I needed spiritual rations more than anything, it seemed.

When back in my cell, in the comforting dark hole, my place of meditation, I recited the rest of chapter eight. "Who shall separate us from the love of Christ? Shall trouble or hardship or persecution or famine or nakedness or danger or sword? As it is written: 'For your sake we face death all day long; we are considered as sheep to be slaughtered.' No, in all these things we are more that conquerors through him who loved us. For I am convinced that neither death nor life," at The Water Cave, "neither angels nor demons," in the operating theater, "neither the present nor the future," under clandestine operation, "nor any powers," of the browbeaters, "neither height nor depth," electric shock or drowning, "nor anything else in all creation." or anything else in all creation, "will be able to separate us from the love of God that is in Christ Jesus our Lord."

That's some love.

So, trust, Sylvia. Trust.

Sixteen
Restaurante de Puma

My stomach growled. It reverberated in the tube, making it sound much louder than reality. The noise reminded me of the soundtrack of an old western movie, where an outlaw shoots a pistol and the bullet pelts a rock, *Ping!*, and then another, *Ding!* echoes. Zip, clink, silence. Weapon cocked again, the resonance of the slug ricocheting, I'd turn pink if in another environment, say, a small church's Bible study group.

Revolting from my negligence in consuming my full ration, I turned to my side, pressing my tummy. The hunger pangs were merciless.

"Lord, I'm sorry I didn't eat when I should have, but I thought you wanted me to pray. So, a little extra food would be nice." I chuckled at the unlikely request, in spite of myself.

Sighing, I tried not to think about hamburgers and French fries, dark chocolate brownies, spaghetti and garlic bread, or fresh, crisp, mixed green salad...

Baked chicken and mashed potatoes, lasagna, blackberry pie...

Green beans—I *love* green beans, corn on the cob, toaster pastries, a hot cup of tea with real cream and sugar...

Ooh, and burritos—without beans and rice, though. I've had about all I could take of those staples. I'd fill it instead with chicken and vegetables, seasoned with cumin and cilantro...

Rosemary based pot-roast, turkey and all the trimmings...

A monster suddenly roared in my domain. The walls of the metal piping might have bent under its duress (darned tummy). Well, so much for not dwelling on food.

The images I conjured took effort to block. Wouldn't you know that songs popped into my head that referred to food? Things like banana boats, bread and butter, a very American apple pie, wanting cornflakes so badly I wished I were one, chocolate covered sunrises, barbecue egg foo yung, something frutti and tutti, paradise with an onion slice on a cheeseburger—it all jingled in my head until I laughed heartily, having a good old side-splitter. Then I heard the wheel on the outer part of the door at my feet turn. My cell opened.

The guard tapped the metal edging twice, my signal to scoot out. The tunnel's lamps emitted light dimmer than usual, which meant the middle of the night. At this hour, the water trickling down the far walls seemed more audible. I waited for the other prisoners to join me, but the guard motioned me to follow him without releasing the others. My stomach dropped, delivering a punch of sickness. What's up with this?

Led to the operating theater, I started to dread what lay ahead. I thought we were over this. I thought this ended, this, this, middle-of-the-night-treatment.

After we turned the dungeon of doom's corner and stumbled into its corridor, I almost planted my nose against the guard's back when he stopped. He whisked his arm, gesturing for me to enter the room without him, although he waited there for me to cross the threshold. I did so with uncertainty. This was all very odd. It's interesting to think one can grow accustomed to procedure, even inhumane *modus operandi*.

I stepped in. The walls looked different. They hadn't changed. I think I had.

In a very methodical manner, Puma, who had been perusing something on the workbench, turned around. He glanced down, ambled passed me and shut the door, locking it.

Uh-oh.

He walked past me again, this time brushing my arm gently. He pulled out a green canvas bag, and then a towel out of the bag. Unfolding the towel, he held a plate in his hand. Pulling the covering, he moved to set the plate down on a small table in the corner, slid a chair up next to it, and gestured for me to sit.

The smell tantalized my senses, made my mouth water. Did he want me to eat that? Then I questioned the possibility of poison.

My jaw dropped. Couldn't seem to keep from gaping, or know how to respond.

"Sit. Eat," he said.

I felt my mouth quiver. I shook my head. "If I...r-refuse...a-are you going to...to torture me?"

Puma hung his head. Pinching his nose, he sighed. He swiped a hand over his face. "It is not poisoned. Here, you see?" With a fork, he took a bite of chicken, of potatoes, of green beans...*my* green beans. "See? Here, okay?"

"W-why?" It came out barely a whisper.

"Uh," he sighed again, "you look too thin." He shrugged, as if he didn't have a good answer.

"Why would you care? I mean, isn't that what you people want, to waste us away to nothing?"

This time he gaped. His head moved from left to right to left to right in slow, precise wags. "We will not speak of these things. It is," he tilted his head, "complicated."

"Complicated?" Sarcasm dripped on my word.

"*Sí*." He chewed the inside of his cheek.

I huffed, yet on the verge of tears, I stood immobile. His image grew blurry.

"Sylvia…"

"Two-five-four!" I spewed through my gritted teeth. "I am prisoner number two-five-four. You erased my name when you, when you…" I gasped.

"Sit," he said.

"No," I cried.

"Sit." The command of his voice made me fly to the chair in an instant.

There I sat staring at the plate of delectable food with tears running down my cheeks.

Puma huffed, and then he released a pent-up incredulous laugh, as if the circumstances played on him as much as they did me. He rubbed his face with both hands this time. Then he tugged his pant legs up a bit before he sat down in an adjoining chair.

"Eat," he whispered.

I picked up the fork. It wavered in my trembling hand. Trying to scoop a green bean, it fell off the utensil numerous times. The tears coursing down my face wouldn't cease. I gave up on the green beans and moved to the chicken, but couldn't cut it. Strength failed me. I was so weak I couldn't cut into a piece of tender meat. I set the fork down, folded my hands in my lap and stared at them, wondering what would happen next.

What did ensue surprised me.

Speechless, I watched as Puma grabbed the green canvas bag again, removed a knife and proceeded to cut my chicken into bite-size pieces, as well as my potato. He speared a piece of poultry and a couple of green beans and then handed them to me.

As I held the fork, he wiped the knife off and placed it back in the bag, tossing the canvas behind the chair. Crossing his arms, he nodded for me to consume the bite he provided me.

I wrapped my mouth around the chicken and green beans. At first, I almost gagged. Then, I closed my eyes to savor the seasoning, the juicy morsel. After only a few chews, I resorted to gulping the bite down. The remainder of the fare I devoured. Afterward, I felt shame for behaving like a glutton. Then the tears started again.

"Do not," he said with a shake of his head, "do not cry." He brushed one side of my cheek with his fingers. Then he gently pulled my chin over to him; with handkerchief in hand, he wiped the moisture from my face.

"Why are you doing this?" I asked. "Acting so nice?" This time I let out a whimper.

"No, sh-sh-sh..." he quieted me. "Yes, this, all of this, is difficult to...comprehend, to sort, uh?"

I nodded.

"*Sí*, well..." he sighed, "I do not wish to hurt you, you understand?"

"B-but you do…"

"I did…"

"And so now you won't?" I said with sarcasm. "What's changed this?"

"Truth."

I snorted. "I don't understand."

He nodded with his head inclined, pensive. "So, maybe you will...in time."

"You can't just tell me?"

"I am not at liberty…"

"No, *I'm* the one not at liberty!" I slapped my hand against the tabletop. "Or have you forgotten?"

Puma didn't answer.

"I did nothing wrong."

He glanced away.

We lingered in silence.

"So," Puma stood. "It is time for you to go back now."

"What about the others?" I asked.

"What about the others?" His brow furrowed.

"Do they get a nice meal, a private audience?"

"This," he motioned between us, "occurred on my personal time. I am not on duty, not following orders by feeding you, you understand." He crossed his arms.

I glanced at the spotted floor. There was a time not long ago where the notion of eating in such a horrid room would have flipped my stomach over and back. I wouldn't have been able to do it. Now, I grew accustomed, desensitized to a degree. "I feel guilty."

Laughter burst from him. "You...feel guilty?" He paused, then exploded in another fit of hilarity.

Because his behavior was always so serious-natured, Puma's sudden amusement stunned me.

When his chuckling quieted, he said, "I do not care about the others." His voice became steel.

"Why not? I mean, why feed me?" I'm not sure I actually wanted to find out.

He inhaled deeply, "Ah, Sylvia," he held his hands up in surrender, and cleared his throat. "Two-five-four," he acquiesced. "Do not question." He sucked in a breath through his teeth. "Do not question." He delivered a glance hard to reckon.

Grateful to have my stomach filled, I searched for the words to thank Puma for the food. They never came. Though he provided the victuals of his own free will, I didn't want to thank *him*.

Back in my cell, I pondered the experience of dining at *Restaurante de Puma*. While I'd give the ambiance less than one star—in fact, the place could use a remodel, a complete overhaul—the cuisine I'd give a full five stars. Now, the service proved inconsistent, for I had frequented before and you never knew what you were going to get. Today, the waitstaff outdid its usual performance. Exemplary, I'd consider returning. However, the next time, if there was a next time, could transpire differently. One just never knew.

Seventeen
Closer, Farther

As much as one could in a tube, I tossed and turned. I had a stomachache from Puma's meal, too difficult to digest after not having real food for a length of time. I hoped upon hope the guards would let us out to stretch and get to the café soon. I needed to use the bathroom. It called my name, first middle and last, like the cawing of a crow. *SPA, SPA, SPA!*

My eyelids beat repeatedly in the pitch-blackness. It was especially humid, so much so I could hardly catch a breath in the tube. My abdomen popped and twisted with endless gurgles. "Stupid chicken," I whispered, blaming the richness of the meal for such bloating.

Feeling disgusted with myself, I needed to purge, both physically and spiritually. Since I had a disadvantage in the physical department in that I couldn't use the bathroom when I needed to, I began to focus on the spiritual. I prayed, asking Jesus to guard my heart and mind.

In a strange way, I felt reproach for getting tetchy about the chicken dinner. Puma provided something very nice, something I hadn't had for a while. And I had asked God for this through my silly visions, vocalizations and songs about all the different things to eat. I experienced such hunger I thought I'd gnaw my way through the metal piping, better than a rat.

"Bathroom, please, please, please, please..." I huffed. "I'm going to explode. Spontaneous human combustion. Yeah, that's it," I laughed until tears leaked from the corners of my eyes. That's not a good thing to do, though. It relaxes certain parts of the body when I needed to clench.

The wheel turned on my tube's door. A guard tapped my foot with his baton, the signal to scoot out. They were releasing the others as well. It took a few minutes. I did the potty dance. Puma, who happened to be in the midst, motioned for me.

"Are you ill?" he asked.

"I have to use the bathroom."

"Come with me."

He led me away from the prisoner's community bathroom at the café. I started to fret until he entered a narrow hallway and stopped outside a tiny cubicle. A toilet sat in the back in the middle, a porcelain throne on which to pay homage.

I started to close the door, but he stopped it with his foot.

"Privacy?" I asked, sheepishly.

He shook his head. "I am sorry, no."

"Ah, who cares?" I almost dove onto the vessel like nobody's business. Whatever needed to exit my body was going to at that moment, whether I wanted it to or not.

Relief came, but almost on its heels came shame on displaying bathroom fireworks in front of someone, even Puma, who had already witnessed me at my worst. Embarrassment over basic things still existed somewhere deep within. As horrible as the moment sounded, I was pleased to find I was still human.

I gained my feet and glanced at him tentatively. He stared at the floor. I moved past him, whispering, "Thank you," as I did so.

Puma nodded and silently led me back to the café where the guards had herded the others and then he disappeared.

I thanked God for relief.

Darío, a wiry fellow, complained of not having enough food during our time in the café. After a few bites, I offered him mine, wondering if it was a wise thing to do. After my stomach troubles, I couldn't eat anyway. He took it without an utterance of thanks and devoured it in a matter of seconds. I turned my eyes away after a sharp pang of guilt.

Allowed to linger in the café for longer than usual, I made good with the bathroom until I knew I didn't need it anymore.

Back in the cell, you'd think I would have resumed my disintegrating existence, but new life breathed into me. Scripture came to life. I had something, something to cling to. Verses took shape in ways I had never known. Imagination grew strong, as did Biblical characters. Although taught to seek comfort in God's word, it never meant what it did at this moment. This was all I had to draw from and I was grateful.

At some point, after I had fallen asleep, the wheel turned on my tube. Instead of a baton, I felt a warm hand on the sole of my left foot. I scooted out and sleepily wavered on my feet, blinking at Puma. He motioned for me to follow.

Other than the soft sound of trickling water, stillness consumed the cave.

I stared at the pack flung over his shoulder.

We passed the silent operating theaters, entered another cave, a smaller tunnel. Having to go single file, he gestured for me to walk in front of him. Anxiety fluttered in my bosom. I don't know why, since we had gone beyond the torture chambers. Perhaps the excursion was reminiscent of the one at the hotel before they abducted me.

I stopped at the end of the hall, staring at the door stationed in front of my nose. Puma reached around me and opened it. When I didn't move, he splayed his arm, indicating he wanted me to pass through. I took a step and then another. Cool, yet sweet air caressed my face, teased my nostrils. I inhaled deeply. Strands of hair tickled my forehead. When I opened my eyes, I took in a clear night sky where the stars appeared so close I could cup one in my hand.

Puma warned me not to take many more steps. That's when I realized the pipeline let us out onto a cliff. The silhouette of the mountains teased my eyes. I longed to see their beauty, but I'd settle for the fresh air. I missed the pleasure of a moment outside. Almost lost in the experience, I remembered Puma. A faint light flickered behind me. I whirled to face him with the sudden fear that he might push me off the edge, even though he did caution me.

Puma had lit a small lantern. He proceeded to unravel his pack, pulling out containers. He piled a plate with food. It looked like…meat…and…

"*Fritanga*," Puma said. "Grilled meat, fried potatoes, *arepas*…" He started to slice up a huge mango. "I hope it

114

is not too rich," he fluttered his fingers. "For your stomach, you know?" He lifted the plate toward me. I hesitated, but it seemed he'd freeze in that position until I took it from him.

I almost dropped it, as weighted as the plate was. He took it back and gestured to sit. When I settled on the rocky ledge, Puma handed it to me again.

The warm food sat in my lap, under my nose. "Oh, it smells so good, but I'm afraid it'll go right through me again." Even as I said it, I knew I was still going to eat it.

Puma gave me a single, authoritative nod. "I will make sure you have access to a lavatory in the morning. Eat." He stuck a fork in my hand, something he let me use during his last meal, but I hadn't seen in a while. We occasionally got spoons at the café, but other than that, hands worked well. They had to.

I had difficulty cutting some of the meat. "I don't suppose I could get a knife..." I already knew his answer, but had to ask anyway.

He shook his head side to side.

I shrugged and used my hands when necessary, consuming half of it before I knew it.

About three bites remained when Puma said, "I, uh, I am s-s..."

The S's disintegrated. Puma, who had casually hung his arms over his knees as he sat on the ground, had also hung his head.

I feared talking to him. The stillness, in addition to my treacherously pounding heart, crippled my tongue. I stared at the man who rocked slightly.

Suddenly he lifted his head, and said, "I am sorry for what has happened to you."

That angered me. My tongue miraculously became whole. "You mean you're sorry for what *you* did to me." I set the plate down.

He hung his head again.

"What did you say?" I couldn't interpret his quiet, mumbled words that slurred together.

"It was a mistake. You..." he cleared his throat. "I made a mistake."

The admission startled me. I didn't know what to feel. Hope crept in my heart and grew overbearing in an instant. "Then let me go," I whispered, desperate tears presenting themselves.

Puma rubbed his face with his hands and stood looking out into the dark mountainous landscape. He clasped his sides, elbows out. After a lengthened pause, he turned from his stance and said, "I would, but...cannot."

"Why?" I demanded.

"It is complicated." He huffed. Puma rubbed his chin, his eyes and then his short-cropped wavy hair with exasperated strokes, his actions reeking of stress.

"Just...just let me go," I whimpered. "It's doesn't have to be complicated." I stood when he continued shaking his head to my every word. "If it's a matter of others knowing about this, I won't tell anyone—I won't tell a soul." I gripped his sleeve. "Please, *please...*" I started sobbing and crumbled back down to the ground.

Puma began putting things into his pack. He straightened. "It is time to go back."

Trapped within the confines of my dreary tube, I started to ask God for understanding but a specific passage slipped out of my mouth instead. The recitation poured out in a pregnant hush, *"The Lord is my shepherd; I shall not want..."*

In the days following, Puma fulfilled his word by ordering a guard to let me out in the mornings so I could use the lavatory. He also fed me regularly at night, after things grew quiet in the pipeline, other than sounds from the operating theater on occasion. I daresay I filled my skin out a little better. We didn't talk much during my dining at *Restaurante de Puma*. It wasn't as if he befriended me and we could gab about superfluous things. No, I was his penance.

In a fit of my own guilt, for eating regular food, receiving special privileges, I once asked Puma, "What about the others?"

"What about them?" he responded coldly.

"Do the other prisoners get special food, a sweater," I tugged on the pullover he let me wear when we were together on an especially cold night.

"The other prisoners deserve their treatment here."

I blinked. "Nobody deserves this."

"Really?" Puma challenged with a hard stare. "I think if you knew the truth of matters, you would disagree."

I shrugged. "I just know that at one point you were convinced I deserved it…" my words fell.

"It has become evident you are…not…like…they are." It seemed painful for him to say that. It came off his tongue like a slice of ice.

I scrunched my face. "What changed?"

"It became clear to me early on. During your," he cleared his throat, "interrogation." He coughed.

"Do the others think so too?"

"Who do you refer to?" Puma glanced at me.

"The other," I cleared *my* throat, "interrogators."

He looked away. "A few are not convinced, but…most understand what happened in your case. I believe those who are unconvinced are only trying to justify their deeds. They know you are innocent." He laughed incredulously. "They know," he finally said with conviction.

I almost didn't want to ask. "So what happens to me now?"

He could have started a fire in the ground by the penetration of his heated eyes. "I do not know." Puma sighed and shifted some papers around on the desk.

I opened my mouth to beg, again, for release. Before I could utter anything, he cut me off.

"Enough!" Puma jumped to his feet, fuming. "Enough, okay, of this, this discussion." He threw his hands into the air. "I do not know. I-do-not-know what will come of this, of you." His pacing had an unsettling affect. Puma leaned against the desk, crossed his arms and stared at me. I could see the ripples of pressure cross his face, the dark and puffy circles under his eyes. "You have become a...an *inconvenience*." He blew a steady stream of air through tightly pressed lips.

I sniffed against the cold. "Why are you even telling me this? I mean, I think it'd be forbidden, against the rules, or something."

"You are correct in your assessment, Sylvia. And I do not know why, other than I think you ought to have an explanation. I owe you that much."

"I'm not sure you've explained anything. I still don't know why, how," I splayed my arms, "I ended up here, enduring your brutality."

Puma didn't flinch in his gaze down at me. He pushed away from the desk and dropped his arms. "I have prayed over your life."

My eyes bugged out. "Prayed?" I asked with cynicism. "You *prayed* for me, over my life, after you've worked so hard to ruin it?" I scoffed. My jaw dropped, but I only made sharp gasps. "I will never recover from this. You have marked me forever," I wept. "Hypocrite," I accused him. "If you pray to God, *my* God," I thumped my chest, "then I don't want to have anything to do with either of you," I sobbed.

Puma's hand found my shoulder. It shook and squeezed at the same time. "There is a lot you do not understand. Still...I am sorry, Sylvia, I am sorry. Please, forgive me..." His begging words shrunk.

I got up and stood by the door, a gesture telling him I wanted to go back to my cell.

With the night's final words, I said to him, "You can kill me if you want to. Have somebody else do it if it somehow absolves you." Bitterness dripped from the sentiment. "Disappear me. I no longer care."

Eighteen
Field of Fate

Privileges vanished. I hadn't seen Puma for days. Back to the once-a-day visit to the café, the grim room with a single picture on the wall, tagged with two doors, I began regretting my last words to my sympathetic torturer.

A few hours after one such visit to the café, two guards came, released me from my tube and led me to a small tunnel I had not seen. They told me to sit against the wall and wait. A few minutes later, another prisoner, a woman wearing a similar denim outfit—only, she had canvas shoes on, entered and sank down next to me. I didn't know her, had never seen her. She couldn't have been older than twenty.

The guards who brought the other woman departed, leaving her and me with my two sentinels who pulled out a deck of cards and started playing, one lighting up a cigarette.

Then I spotted Frick, who wore his usual white sport coat and jeans, waltzing toward us with nonchalance. Puma, head down, trailed behind him.

Unlike Frick, who stared at us, eyes filled with mischief, Puma didn't look at anything but the floor.

"Get up, *señoras*. We are going for a little ride."
Coming from Frick, this could mean anything.

I clasped the hand of the young woman next to me and we shuffled with timidity, facing together, whatever lay ahead. The young woman whispered her name from the corner of her mouth, "Lola."

"Sylvia," I replied.

I don't know why we made this exchange. Perhaps if something happened to one of us, a very real possibility, the survivor would remember the other's name, keep her alive somehow by acknowledgment, a sort of commemoration.

She squeezed my hand. I squeezed hers back.

At the end of the tunnel, the large door opened to a painfully bright shaft of light, the first exposure I'd had to real sunlight in a long while. My eyes watered. I covered them with my hand, but the adjustment didn't come very fast. We were ushered down a ramp, across a crude parking lot and loaded into a truck, Lola and I sandwiched between Frick, who decided to drive, and Puma.

I wondered why they didn't put hoods on us. That was odd, too. Considering they went to great measures to conceal anyone's comings and goings. I'd bite my nails with worry had I still decent nails to bite.

The road trip dragged on. Aside from a nagging feeling that the scenic tour wouldn't amount to what I thought it would in the end, the breathtaking mountains, like low-lying waves of a still and mysterious ocean, captivated. *This* was the Colombia I wanted to be acquainted with, not a clandestine prison.

Over rough, potholed dirt roads, and various switchback descents, the path leveled for a spell. We drove through fields, like pampas, and came to a halt at a meadow that looked eerily familiar. I glanced at the nearby thicket. My heart accelerated.

"Get out," Frick ordered.

Puma opened his door. I went out his side. Lola exited out of Frick's.

We were ordered to march straight ahead, and then Frick finally stopped us. I could see patches of freshly overturned dirt nearby. A horrible awareness washed over me. *They're going to kill us.*

Frick told Lola and me to remain with our backs turned, but sink to our knees. When I hesitated, his hand—at some point wrapped around cold metal—shoved me down at the shoulder. Without thinking, I placed my hands behind my head until Frick told me to leave them at my sides. *They're going to shoot us and bury us here.* I started hyperventilating. *No one will know. Not my parents, friends—no one!*

Something distracted Frick. It was the usual. He said, "You know, I think I am going to have a little fun with this one first." He pushed Lola to the ground, her face into the earth. She shrieked and fought him, trying to slither away, but you can't very well slither away from a snake. Lola was unaccustomed to Frick's ways, apparently. I started to feel sorry for her, until I glanced over my shoulder at Puma who also held a pistol, which he aimed· at the back of my head.

Fifteen feet away, Frick shouted at Puma to take a little pleasure, too, if he wanted, but do the job. Then he didn't pay any attention to us.

Lola screamed.

I held my violently trembling hands out to Puma. "I-I didn't mean it." Sounds akin to sobbing and gasping combined came out with every breath. I stuttered, "What I said before…I want to live! Please, please don't," I shook my head until it made me dizzy, "don't kill me."

Puma's demeanor crumbled. The pistol started to quiver slightly. He brought his hands to his head and tugged at his hair, grimacing as if screaming silently. Then he pointed the weapon again, the same time I sucked in air.

"Please," I swallowed. "I want to live." I tentatively and fearfully touched the barrel and whispered hoarsely. "Y-you said you pray for me. I pray for you, too. Right now, I pray you let me live!"

Before I could blink, Puma turned me around and pushed, pushed me—hard—toward the thicket. Once within the coverage of jungle, he made me lie flat. He pressed his body against mine while rasping into my ear, "Hide here. Do not move, no matter what you see or hear. I will come for you later." His voice was steelier than the firearm he maneuvered with sudden finesse. Puma sprung to his feet and aimed down.

My whole body flinched when the blast went off.

Though my ears rang, I didn't feel any pain; I could still move. My hands involuntarily patted my body for where the bullet had gone in. I blinked up at Puma who stood staring at me while still pointing the pistol not three feet, but away.

Another shot reverberated. It came from the field.

Lola.

"Do as I say," Puma mouthed more than spoke it.

I nodded emphatically while clutching fists to my face. I clamped my eyes.

Lola didn't make it. I knew it, because I knew the nature of Frick. But then again, Puma had transitioned right before me. Could it be?

Rolling and scooting, I found a peeking place in my new jungle hideout. I could see Puma gesturing for Frick, who had pulled a shovel out of the bed, to get inside the truck. They had an animated conversation. Finally, Frick tossed the shovel back in, its sickening thump even I could hear, in spite of the distance between us, and climbed in the passenger side this time.

Puma started the truck and left a cloud of dirt in its wake, the gears grinding restlessly.

When my perpetrators disappeared from sight, I strained, panting, trying to catch a glimpse of the field, of Lola. Scuffling nearer to the edge, I half stood, although my knees trembled, threatening to buckle altogether. I saw her and drew closer.

She looked at me with glassy, lifeless eyes. Other than the gaping hole in her head and the growing splotch of blood-soaked dirt, like a halo around her crown, she appeared peaceful. Too peaceful, except for the fear forever imprinted on her irises, forever haunting me.

I bent to close her eyelids, only because that's what I had seen actors do in the movies…and because it made it easier to gaze at her. But then I hesitated. Judging from the freshly churned dirt nearby, I guessed I stood on other unmarked graves of political deviants such as I. Someone would return to bury the dead. If Frick returned, he'd notice the downturned eyelids. He'd probably wonder about my remains. I didn't touch her.

Puma came to mind. I wondered what cockamamie story he'd formulate to tell Frick. Would it convince him?

Kneeling beside Lola, I offered a little prayer, but it ended up in a howl of anguish. Sniffing, I lifted my head and stared at a dark orange sky quickly turning black through tear-marred vision. Strange noises grew louder in the thicket, like the jungle coming alive after a long, dormant period.

I clambered back under the cover of green, the boisterous, taunting, restless green—in the woods, right where Puma told me to stay. He didn't mention anything about a creature that sounded like a woman screaming, the howls, chirps, slithers, cracks, and grinds. And the insects—oh man, they'd eat me alive! Something crawled on me every few seconds, and I couldn't see what it was! I couldn't see anything. This environment delivered a fright of its own.

I pulled up into a ball, like a fetus, chilled and shivering, swatting and brushing unknown crawling things off my numbing skin. "God, are you still there?" I muttered, doubting. My voice—I sounded sick.

It seemed half the night passed. A faint hum grew steadier. Lights flashed. I popped up, brushing something hairy off my shoulder. The squeak of brakes and the crank of an emergency brake saved me from my own imagination. Headlights flooded the field. I could make out a figure, but I couldn't tell...

The figure, complete with a wide-beamed flashlight neared the forest. I sank down, heart palpitating. I heard footsteps invade the thicket. The shaft of the flashlight drifted on and off objects.

I heard my name called.

"Puma?" I answered.

"*Sí*. Show yourself. I have come alone..." his eyes drifted over me and then grew wider at my feet. He stepped over, grabbing me quickly and flicked something away with the tip of his boot.

I closed my eyes and whispered, "Should I ask what that was?"

"No," he said with nervous tension.

"Oh."

"You do not want to know."

The curiosity got the better of me and I turned my head, knitting my brows over a tarantula-like looking thing that had its front legs raised, and body erect, as if ready for war. It even swayed back and forth in a stance of dare.

"Um, is it going to spring and attack? I mean, they can't fly or anything..."

Puma pulled on my arm with impatience. "I need your assistance."

"What do you want me to do?"

"Help me dispose of the other prisoner, quickly, before anyone knows what I have done with you here."

"You mean, *not* done...by sparing me?"

He didn't answer.

I followed him back to the truck, content to be out of the infested canopy of jungle. Puma grabbed two shovels out of the bed, extending one toward me.

"You can't be serious?" I said.

He swayed. "It is the least you could do, considering I am disobeying orders by not putting a bullet in your head," he snapped.

My jaw dropped. Then I clamped my teeth together, grabbed the shovel and followed Puma.

We slowed. Puma held his arm out to keep me behind him. The beam from the superpower flashlight showed three bush dogs pulling on Lola's skin.

I shrieked, "Oh, do something! Get them away from her!"

Puma picked up some rocks and pelted the dogs. I did the same, although I missed the wild canines. At last, they yelped and scurried away. Puma positioned the flashlight.

I couldn't look at Lola, eyes open, disfigured, practically scalped. Dropping the shovel and stumbling away, I emptied the contents of my stomach. I detected a pause in Puma's attack against the loose earth, until I caught my breath and straightened my frame. When he resumed, I wiped my mouth, marched to him, grabbed the shovel and moved dirt a little, ignoring Puma's inquisitive gaze.

He pulled the shovel from my hands and flung it a few feet away. "Go sit down over there," he pointed, before he wiped sweat from his brow.

Puma saved my life, yes, but I didn't want to be an accomplice in Lola's unscrupulous murder. I think he knew that. Nevertheless, I had already seen too much. I looked away when it came time to drag Lola's body toward the narrow hole in the ground. Not even six feet under, I wondered if animals would dig these shallow graves up in time.

"How many are buried here?" I asked with the tone of my voice descending.

Puma ignored me. He breathed heavily as he heaved Lola, releasing her body that crumpled into the soil with nothing more than a soft, dull sound. Puma worked double-time to fill the dirt and tamp it down by shovel and boot. He took patches of turf and then long grass and covered the area, making it appear as the other recently churned patches nearby.

"I'm surprised you and Frick don't have people beneath you to do this petty work, you know, the digging and burying and all."

"*Frick?*" He glanced at me questioningly.

"Your partner."

"Ah." He glared. "This time is different."

I exhaled. With sarcasm dripping from my words, I said, "Well, you guys have quite a racket going on here…"

"Shut up! Just shut up!" He sprung on me, gripped my cheeks with one dirt-stained hand. We had a stare down contest.

Air whistled out of Puma's nose. Finally, he softened. Released his hold on me. He gathered the shovels and, head hung, retreated to the truck. Halfway there, he shifted, calling over his shoulder, "Are you coming?"

I closed my eyes, inhaled and exhaled, just to make sure I could still do so, and somehow moved my feet that took me closer to the truck. Then I retreated, as if forgetting something. I quickly hit the ground and grappled for rocks, stacking them into a little makeshift marker. I muttered a quick prayer, recited the 23rd Psalm, and then climbed into the passenger side. The cab seemed too big, almost hollow, with just the two of us.

Hollow. Like my heart.

The engine sparked and revved in a single instant. It made me jump, even in my numbing state.

We drove. I hung on, over potholes, narrow paths barely resembling roads, my hands gripping the edge of the seat.

Eventually, the nightlights of a large city hovered in the nearby horizon, a metropolis dipped down in a valley. I thought we'd enter the city, but Puma kept us on the outskirts.

He turned into a parking lot at the back of a white, industrial-looking building. When he cranked the parking brake and shut off the engine, he told me to stay put.

Puma opened the door of a white car parked next to the truck. I watched him under a dim light retrieve a bundle of something from the back of the car. He tossed it at me in the truck. "Change into these."

I unrolled the bundle of clothes. Oversized pair of cream-colored pants and an oversized thin navy sweater. I didn't know to whom the garments belonged, but I didn't care. They could be Puma's for all I knew. Eager to get the prison denim off, the exchange happened in the blink of an eye. Too bad I still didn't have any shoes.

When Puma saw I had finished, he motioned with his head to get out of the truck and then into the car. We drove again…for hours. Crossed a valley floor, cruised the bridges over numerous rivers that lined with semi-tropical foliage, traversed mountains. The sun rose and we still drove. Puma didn't say a word, wouldn't answer any of my questions; he had decided not to converse. Ignored, I fell asleep.

I don't know how long I was out, but the traffic flow changed. Car horns, beeps, a lot of stopping and starting… I opened my eyes to another city. Something familiar nagged at me.

"Where are we?"

Puma still chose not to talk. When I glanced at him, I noticed the darkening of the already dark circles under his eyes, the veins in his neck protruding. He appeared the epitome of stress. Like a pressure cooker about to explode.

Then a recognizable building caught my eye and I did a double take. Puma slowed to a stop, the brakes rebelling with a little squeak.

The U.S. Embassy.

Bogotá.

Puma hesitated, then shifted in his seat. He wouldn't look at me. He said, "Go inside. You go right in to see a *Señor* Chuck Goren. Talk to nobody else, you understand. Only *Señor* Chuck Goren. He will make the arrangements for you to get home."

Goren's a co-conspirator? I picked at a scab on my arm. "Just like that, huh?"

Puma didn't answer, yet the tendon in his jaw started pulsating. I didn't press him. Pushing my shoulder against the metal to open the car door, Puma said one final thing.

"I never want to see you again, Sylvia." He held his fist against his mouth, moving it only when he spoke. "Do not come to Colombia again."

I share your sentiment. "You have nothing to worry about."

Nineteen
The Meaning of Home, Lost

I marched straight to Chuck Goren's office, clipping past his alarmed secretary, ignoring her warnings to "stop" and "you can't go in there." When I barged in, Mr. Goren's eyes widened. I stood there, dirty, unkempt, donning clothes two times too big and barefoot.

I said, "Remember me? Yeah, that's right. I don't care if you're *understaffed,* nor do I give a rip about your precious *budget cuts.* Issue me a new passport. Get me the proper documentation—and send me on a plane out of here, NOW!"

The coffee-filled paper cup slipped from Mr. Goren's hand, staining the yellow area rug.

He wordlessly did what I asked, to my surprise. I didn't actually think he'd pull it off. I figured excuses or delays would usurp my plans for an expedited journey home. Eight hours later, I sat on a plane after his secretary had given me a change of clothes and shoes, a brush and lip-gloss. It all made me more presentable, I'm sure. I know I must have looked rather ghastly when I pushed my way into Goren's office.

The strangest thing I've ever experienced—sitting on a plane full of people. Travelers laughed, slept, read and watched their movies on portable players. Scrunched against the window, I behaved paranoiac, disconnected with those around me. Life went on—had gone on, while I suffered injustices, the worst abuses. I learned I had spent four months, one week and two days in a clandestine prison referred to as The Water Cave. The detention center, more like a concentration camp, held me for subversive political activities, only I'm apolitical. I've never understood politics and never have had an interest.

I glanced around. How dare these people, these passengers! Didn't they know what I had gone through? What nerve! To carry on and exchange pleasantries when I had endured such vile abuses. My rights as a human had been violated!

And then I wondered if anyone else among the travelers looked like me: hollow, suspicious, clinging to the porthole window like they were freedom itself. I leaned forward in my search for that individual. The man I sat next to met me halfway, blocking my view and asked with a smile in what part of the States I lived. Why did he assume I lived in the U.S.? Nerdy, Melba toast boy, Spencer, lived in Colombia. I clamped my eyes and turned away from the man, sinking back in the corner without a word, other than a sigh laden with sadness.

Making a connecting flight in L.A., getting through customs, I finally landed in Portland, Oregon. I couldn't get on the shuttle to the park-n-ride, because I didn't have the little yellow ticket I obtained when I checked my car in. I wondered what to expect with the parking place, since they anticipated my return after only one week's visit. Would my car still be there? I doubted it. Besides, fatigue overcame me and I didn't have the keys. I hailed a cab, hoping the Visa gift card Goren gave me to use as cash had enough remaining on it to take care of the fare.

The city lights reflected off the Willamette River, a tributary of the Columbia, nothing like a *Colombian* river, as we cruised over the interstate bridge toward Vancouver, my hometown. I expected some great sensation to come over me, some significant emotion. I felt nothing.

My city. My street. My house. Except for the porch light and a sidelight I don't remember leaving on, the little white rancher appeared dark and forgotten.

I sighed, my shoulders rising and falling with a feeling of collapse.

"Take the fare out of this," I handed the driver the Visa gift card, "and see if what's on there can cover it, plus a tip."

"It sure does, ma'am. With probably plenty left over." He handed the card back to me with a smile. After a long pause, he said, "Ma'am?"

"Hm?" I came out of my trancelike numbness. "Oh, right. I'll just...um...thanks for the ride." I finally opened the rear car door so the man could get back to work by picking up another passenger.

"Have a good night," the cabby said.

As soon as I stepped out and shut the door, the taxi drove away, leaving me standing staring at my house, wondering what I was supposed to do next. "I suppose an entry key is in order," I muttered. I coursed around the side and tipped a small urn while holding onto the top, and patted the mulch for the spare I kept hidden. One thing I noticed, even in the dimly lit dark, was how nicely the landscape appeared. Somebody had tended it. I knew my yard well enough that weeds would have choked out

everything else after only a few weeks of my absence.
"Ah, there it is, half buried." The thought startled me. The
last time I touched dirt wasn't around a neat little patch of
shrubs and flowers, but someone's unmarked grave I had
tried to mark.

When I steadied, I stumbled to the front door and
stared at it for the longest time before slipping the key in
the deadbolt and knob.

It felt strange to be inside. I stood in the entryway for
what seemed forever. Then I sighed and tiptoed forward
as if the house belonged to somebody else. A nightlight in
the hallway lit the Berber-carpeted floor, and when I
entered the living room and peered straight ahead into the
kitchen, I saw the light over the stove on as well.

Cleaner than when I do the required chores myself, the
house sat tidy and neat—so neat, it almost hurt my nose to
sniff the glass cleaner and wood polish that still hung in
the air.

The fridge contained an assortment of fresh food. I
flicked on the lights over the dining nook. Stacks of flyers
spread over the modest table. "Missing," the heading said,
along with a two-year-old photograph of me, contact
information, and a reward for details pertaining to my
whereabouts.

Normally my heart would have sunk into my stomach,
but I had no feeling, experienced no emotion. Completely
numb, I was a stranger in this home. I sighed and opened a
manila folder. The same flyers, but printed in Spanish,
popped out at me. The contact information appeared the
same, except for one primary addition, a woman's name,
Laura Aguilera, who resided in Colombia. I didn't know
who she was. I closed the folder.

Creeping through the rest of the house, I poked my head in the attached garage where my red sedan sat. "Back from the park-n-ride safe and sound, I see." Shutting that door, I stumbled into the bedroom and glanced around. Why did everything appear so foreign? I rubbed my temples.

In spite of the detached sensation I experienced, a certain familiarity touched a piece of my fragmented heart. The only one who would have kept my personal things shipshape, expecting my return at any time, believing in it…

Mom. ·

Twenty
Whatever's Next

"Oh God, Oh God, thank you, Jesus!"

The shriek pulled me out of my comatose slumber. I stirred under the smothering embrace of my mother who wept and rocked me awake as if I weighed five hundred pounds, while patting me gently as if I were a baby. A giant infant metamorphosed into a desperate woman who depended on the maternal instincts that overwhelmed me. I squeezed her, as if wringing out a wet towel, and we huddled on the bed, finally collapsing, a pile of pathetic hyenas.

After who-knows-how-long, Mom stroked my tear-streaked face, brushing strands of hair behind my ears. "Look at you. Where did you go off to?" she wept. "Your father and I searched everywhere. We even went to Colombia."

"You did?"

"Yes," she wiped her nose with her wrist.

"Did you find Spencer?"

She shook her head, tousling her short gray hair while releasing a loud exhale. "The language institute wasn't much help. We managed to drag information out of a woman at the information desk, and she told us Spencer no longer taught at the school. That she hadn't seen him in months."

"When did you go to Bogotá?"

"Three months ago." She sighed heavily. "When we realized you didn't just fly off for a spontaneous vacation." Mom looked at me squarely. "When the auto pound started sending notices to claim your car their towing company removed from the park-n-ride." Her face crinkled again. "I'm so glad you're here. Don't you know you made me sick with worry?" She grabbed me and tightened her hug. "My baby girl is home," my mother crooned.

When we pulled apart, my shoulders slumped. "I saw the flyers," I said. "You dispersed them around here, too."

"Of course we did. We didn't want to leave any stone unturned. But I knew you went to Colombia. I found the flight itinerary in your Inbox on the computer. I checked everywhere for a possible message from you. So what happened?"

I cleared my throat. "Did you go to Spencer's house?"

She nodded. "The place was untouched. Like he stepped away and vanished, just like that."

"Untouched?" I furrowed my brows, seeing Spencer's home ransacked with vivid recollection.

"Yes," she rubbed the front of her neck, something she did when nervousness hit her. "I don't suppose you have any idea of his whereabouts?"

I had guessed his fate, but hoped he'd show up one day just as I did for my mom. She studied my face. Mom took my hands between hers and examined them. I quickly pulled them away and wrapped my hands around my girth.

"How about some coffee? I'll put a pot on." She stood and pulled me up with her. Draping her arm over my shoulders, she led me into the kitchen and sat me down at the table in the nook. I glanced out the window. Darkness still monopolized the sky. I shivered.

"What time is it?" I asked, something I hadn't done or needed to do since my capture.

"Six." My mom slipped a pastel pink cardigan over my shoulders. She shuffled to the sink, where the faucet discharged water into a carafe for the coffeemaker.

"In the morning?"

"Yes." Mom fed water into the machine. It started crackling from water drips on the heating plate, as it grew hot. Then sputters and groans followed. The smell of coffee made my mouth water.

"Is this what you've done every morning?" I suspected her answer.

She said, "Every morning, afternoon and evening. I hoped every day to hear news of you, to see you walk through that door." She pointed in the direction of the entryway. "Then, when I found you lying on the bed, on top of the covers and all, it scared me. Because I know how much you like to burrow in the blankets to sleep. I couldn't raise you, and so I thought you were dead. But then you moaned." She pulled two brown mugs out of the cabinet, "Ah! What a glorious sound that was, I tell you what." Mom turned and smiled with sadness evident on her face. She had aged since I saw her last.

I sighed like an elephant and pulled the soft pink cardigan tighter around my torso.

Mom poured the coffee and set a mug in front of me. I wrapped my hands around it, allowing the warmth to infiltrate my skin. She sank down in the seat across from me with questions in her eyes. One slipped out. "So, what's next?"

Twenty-one
Residue

Things aren't always better with time.

I heard the knocking that turned to pounding on the door, yet I couldn't bring myself to answer it. When I heard a key inserted into the lock with a quick grind and a frantic burst inside, I knew my worried mom wouldn't let me be. She'd find where I had hidden; she did every time.

"Sylvia! Sylvia, answer me," she shouted, panic manifested in her voice.

A few thumps later, she opened the door to the vacuum closet that had sheltered me. I glanced up at her from my new dark shell.

She expelled her breath in a way that made me deeply sorry for consuming her with worry. It wasn't intentional. I couldn't seem to help it.

"The closet today," she said, "yesterday under the bed, the day before that I found you in the shower with the bathroom lights off and the fan on. How long is this going to go on? It's been two months! How long are you going to do this to yourself?"

My face turned hot. It crumpled.

"And what about your management job at the marketing firm? Vicky held your position, waiting for you to come back, until she couldn't hold it anymore. She told me this morning she finally had to replace you, that you haven't even stopped in there to talk to her! Everybody is moving on but you."

I let out a sob and hid my head between my knees.

My mother squatted with a grunt. She placed a hand on my knee. With a softened voice, she asked, "What happened to you, baby girl?"

After a spell of deep-seated weeping, I choked out the words, "My heart hurts so much. I wonder how it can keep beating inside. Sometimes I think it would be better for everyone if it just stopped."

"No, no, no," my mom pulled me into her arms. "Oh, don't say that, don't say that," I heard her voice tremble. I knew she tried to be strong, but worry overwhelmed her. She sounded scared.

I pulled back. "At the same time my heart hurts, it's also very hollow. It's like I don't know who I am anymore," I gasped.

"You need help. You need professional help."

I shook my head.

"Yes, yes you do, Sylvia. You can't go on like this." She squared my shoulders and gripped them like a vise. "Your father knows someone. We'll set you up with an appointment."

When I thought of communicating to anyone, I shrunk with shame. I don't know why, but I felt shame. None of this was my fault. Was it?

"Come on. Get up. You need to do this for yourself and if not for yourself, then for us."

The sternness of her words scared me. I scooted farther back into the closet.

.

"No, you don't. Come out of the closet this instant, you're scaring me!"

"Mom, I am sorry," I whimpered. "I am so sorry, but I can't...I can't..."

"Fine."

"What are you doing?"

"What do you think I'm doing? If you're not going to come out, then I'm sitting in here with you." She tried to squeeze in.

"There's not enough room."

My mom tried so hard to get her body in the vacuum closet we suddenly burst out laughing.

"Maybe we should go into slapstick," I suggested.

She chuckled and managed to put her arm around my shoulders. "Yes...maybe." She patted me and began rocking while humming a gentle old hymn. I recognized the melody, *O Thou in Whose Presence*.

Mom started singing, "Say, why in the valley of death should I weep, or alone in this wilderness rove. Oh why should I wander an alien from thee, and cry in the desert for bread..."

"Mom?"

"Yes, baby girl?"

"I'm a good person, right?"

"Oh, of course you are," she said, rocking me with a little more sway.

I opened my mouth, but words failed me. Stuttering, it finally slipped out, "Something very bad happened to me."

The deadened silence frightened me, especially when the comforting sway ceased. Finally, a firm, "I know."

"I keep asking God 'Why.' All my life I've tried to do the right things. I went to church, I did my devotions, I treated others as I wanted to be treated. Why did this happen to me?"

"Bad things sometimes happen to good people." She pulled away and looked at me. "You know the story your father and I taught you, that with the fall of man came endless sin, death, disease, and destruction. With evil unleashed in the world, the hardness of people's hearts enabled the infliction of injury one toward another. Christ gave us light and life and freedom, but he also gave us a choice."

I huffed. "But I chose him, and I suffered terrible things, Mom. Where was he then? I thought He was supposed to protect me?"

"He promises eternal life, but the foul things of this world belong to this world. Our bodies can be harmed, but not our souls—they belong to him."

"Mom, it just seems...so unfair."

"It is. There is a purpose with everything. You don't need to figure that out on your own, or right now, for that matter. Lean on the Lord, Sylvia." She took a lacey hanky and dabbed my eyes, and then her own before she blew her nose in it. "I've been trying to get you to go to church. I want to see you there, but if you're not ready, you're not ready. You're stubborn, and I have this feeling that even though your father and I schedule you to see a psychologist, you won't go." She sounded exasperated. "So, right now, find something that comforts you, something that reflects God's grace, and saturate yourself in it." Mom pulled me out of the closet and we stood to our feet. "When was the last time you've eaten?"

I wagged my head. "Days, hours, time has all blurred into nothing. I honestly don't know when I ate last."

She wrapped her hands around my arm and pulled me down the hall toward the kitchen. "I'm going to make you something…"

"I'm not hungry…"

"I wasn't asking." She sat me down in the nook. "I'm going to make you food and you're going to eat it. When I know you've had enough, I want you to stay away from the closets and dark places in the house. Turn on the lights for a change. Move about. I'll board up all of your hideouts if I have to, but you are no longer going to retreat into these dungeons you've created for yourself."

Glaring at her, I said, "*I* didn't create them, somebody else did."

"That's where you're wrong," she said with austerity in her voice. "You are making the decisions now, regardless of what anybody else did to you. And they are poor choices, Sylvia."

"Don't you dare blame me," I bawled.

"No, no, no, no, no—that's not what I said." She came over and leaned, draping her body over mine. "I am not blaming you for whatever happened, nobody is. But you have to make a change. And you know what? Forget about making decisions. Let God make them for you. You need to lean on him right now. Right now, Sylvia. You are alive, you are home, and you have a future. It's time to move toward it with hope. Start over if you need to, but begin by taking a step. One step. Don't worry about more than that. Just take one step, that's all your mother asks of you."

I tried to nod my head, but I only saw my uncombed hair that hid part of my face quiver.

"Okay?" She faced me. "Okay?" Mom said with even more firmness.

"Okay," I whispered.

"I'm praying for God to intervene, but you have to meet him partway. Take that step." She went back to fixing soup and sandwiches.

We ate in silence. When I pushed the plate and bowl away after a few bites, she wagged her head and pushed it back in front of me. I managed to consume most of it.

Sitting back with a puff, pressing my hands against my stomach, I gazed out the window. The sun fought through the overcast skies and won. I stared at the striped rays running across my small side yard. That's my life right now, I thought. There are these beams of light reminiscent of the faith I once had trying to break through the bleak, grey clouds that have engulfed me. Focusing on the light, it disappeared as billows moved, covering the sun. But then it reappeared, and when it did the rays spread and joined like one wave. In a moment, the entire area lit up with bright, white light. It blinded me. I looked away.

After my mom cleared the dishes, rinsed them and put them in the dishwasher, she gave me a kiss on the top of my head. "Find something to comfort you today. I'll check on you later."

She shuffled out of the house, the front door clicking behind her.

The sun warmed the nook, warmed me. I closed my eyes and let it saturate me. My skin tingled. I rubbed it. Then I got up and paced from room to room. At some point, I began humming the hymn my mom had sung to me in the closet. I knew then what I wanted to do.

Going over to the shelves in the living room, I fingered through my collection until I found it. Pulling the CD out, I placed it in the player, delivering a gentle tap against the flat door and the arm closed, taking *This Bright Hour* with it.

"...find something that comforts you, something that reflects God's grace, and saturate yourself in it," Mom had said.

I hit the Seek button until I found it. Then I set the song to play continuously. Fernando Ortega crooned a haunting rendition of the hymn.

Lying on the floor, I draped my arm over my eyes to ward against the lights that were still on, and I listened. Even after I shut off the player, the depth of the music penetrated my soul. I started to sing the old hymn aloud, this time the way I had learned it as a child, in the new quiet of my living room. "Oh Thou in whose presence my soul takes delight, on whom in affliction I call; My comfort by day and my song in the night, my hope, my salvation, my all..."

I wept. Hard. From the pit of my stomach. "God, I need your help," I whispered. "Restore me, I ask—I beg."

Singing turned to humming, turned to settling peace. I didn't sleep, didn't think, didn't do anything but loll, basking in the beauty of the song's meaning.

Later that evening, I took a shower, worked the knots out of my hair and threw on a pair of beige Dockers, a brown sweater and comfortable penny loafers.

Staring at my red sedan that glanced back at me in a dare, I took a long, deep, steadying breath. "I can do this," I whispered.

The first time I had been out of the house since Colombia, I hit the button on the remote, which the visor held by a clip. The garage door opened. I started the car, allowing it to warm up for what seemed like forever. At last, I put the gear in reverse, pulled out and headed in the direction of church before I changed my mind.

Twenty-two
Human Rights Retributive Board of Colombia

"I'm so glad to see you doing better, baby girl. I admit you had me on some kind of scare."

"I didn't mean to hurt you, Mom." I gazed at the beads of condensation dripping down the glass holding my soda, which the waitress had already refilled once.

"I know. I'm just glad you have finally crossed the threshold to healing." Mom took another bite of her grilled salmon.

Nodding, I said, "Church has helped, getting reconnected." I played with the wild rice around my filet of blackened tilapia. "It took six months," I snorted.

"Hey, you're doing great. Some people go on years without seeking help. It's sad, because there is hope for folks out there. I think between attending church, therapy with Dr. Nell, getting out in public, your own effort to change—it all helps. I am very proud of you."

I stared at my hands that fell in my lap. "I'm better, but I still feel like I have... I don't know," I sighed. "I still wake up screaming sometimes."

Mom took a drink of her water, scrutinizing me over the rim of her glass. "You'll get there. One step at a time, remember?"

"Yeah," I exhaled, playing with the tip of my napkin.

Chewing, my mom said, "And what about employment? Have you..." she left it unasked.

"No, I haven't looked." I stuttered, "I spoke with Vicky, though. There's a chance she can find a placement for me in their sister office. But, I don't really want to commute an hour each way to Salem." I shrugged. "But...I guess I can't afford to be choosy."

"Look around." She brought the white linen to her mouth and wiped the rest of the faded pink from her lips. "I'm sure something will work out. You're not a slouch."

I laughed. It felt good. Then I decided to finish the rest of my meal after all.

When we walked to Mom's car, she said, "I've been waiting until I thought you were ready. There's someone I want you to meet."

"Who?"

"Her name is Laura Aguilera."

Something triggered my mind, telling me I knew this name. Squinting, it finally came to me. "The 'woman missing' flyers, the ones that you used in Colombia."

"Yes. Laura has become a friend of mine. She lives part of the time in the U.S., in Portland and the other part in Bogotá. She made connections while in Colombia to help find you. The woman works around the clock, I tell you."

"What does she do?"

"She's with the Human Rights Retributive Board of Colombia. Ever since you showed up, she's been eager to meet with you, but you were just so fragile..."

"I still am..."

"Not like you were." We got into the car. Mom put the key in the ignition, but paused. "Laura has unearthed new evidence she has been desperate to talk to you about. She's called me literally every day."

My curiosity piqued; at the same time, familiar dread balled in my stomach. What would I discover, and how would I face it? I feared to ask, but did all the same, "When do we meet?"

"I'd like to take you over there now."

My gulp audible, I slipped out an, "Okay."

My mom squeezed my knee, patted it and then turned the key to start the ignition. "You are not alone anymore."

We drove across the bridge in silence, the Columbia River appearing windswept. Small whitecaps surfaced in sporadic formation. We ventured well into the city and found parking on a side street lined by a row of shabby buildings. Not the nicest area of the city, it also was not the worst.

After feeding the parking meter, we traipsed a half block until we came to a brown building. A sign hanging at the side of the door listed various businesses. I saw something pertaining to human relations and a commission of human rights.

Up the stairs of a musty smelling building, revealing its age, we stopped on the second floor, walked through a door, down a short hall that our shoes clip-clopped down on the linoleum floor, and came to a light wood-framed door with a window. An 8 ½ X 11 piece of paper scotch-taped in the center of the window listed three names of people in that particular office. Laura Aguilera was one of them.

I practiced breathing all the way to Laura's desk where she glanced up at us. When it dawned on her that her friend Cathi had successfully brought her daughter in and I was

standing right in front of her, Laura jumped out of her chair
and about leaped over her desk.

She clasped my hands, shaking them vigorously, and
kissed me on the right cheek. "So nice to meet you—
finally," she exclaimed. "Welcome, welcome…"

"It's nice to meet you, too, Ms. Aguilera, I mean *Señora*
Aguilera."

"No, please, call me Laura." She led me to the back that
narrowed, past other office doors, and to an area that
opened up to a sort of backroom and refreshment center.
Mom followed.

"Coffee?"

"Sure." I barely detected a Latin accent. "Were you
raised in Colombia?"

"I was born there. In Medellín."

I thought of Gloria.

"Cream, sugar?"

"Black is fine. Thank you," I said when she handed me
the Styrofoam cup. She handed a cup to my mom that
included the perfect amount of cream. I surmised they had
met often.

She gestured to a ratty couch, perfect for a break room.
"Please, come, sit with me," her low, deep voice
commanded.

We didn't chitchat long. I broke the niceties. "Laura,
why did you want to speak with me?"

Lowering her cup, she cocked her head and examined
me. "I know you feel shame, and you should not. I know
you feel isolated, stripped of identity, and you will heal,
just as your body has healed." She glanced at my fingers.
"You are Sylvia Abbott, and you have a voice. You do not
have to hide it any longer."

I set my cup down to her pointed statements and crossed my arms. "What is this about?" I studied Laura, her pepper and silver-streaked hair, white cardigan over a light blue cotton shirt, denim skirt that made me cringe, and Birkenstocks.

She set her coffee down too. "We need your help."

"You need *my* help...for what?"

Her shoulders rose and fell. "Sylvia, I am sure Cathi filled you in on who I work for...?"

"The Human Rights Retributive Board of Colombia."

"Yes. Here, come with me..." She stood and ambled to the very back where three long tables were pushed together to form a U-shape. Laura and I stood in the middle. My mom lingered in the shadows.

The tables had stacks of papers, photos spread out, and manila files and envelopes. It looked like a mess, and at the same time, some sort of order existed.

"Sylvia...," she addressed me with heaviness. "In Colombia, you were apprehended and tortured—am I correct in this statement?"

Dizziness attacked. The room threatened to collapse and disappear. "I-I need to sit down," I mumbled.

"Of course." She pointed to something. "Cathi?"

My mom brought over a metal foldout chair. I crumbled into it, stretching my head back, eyes closed. After the lightheadedness dissipated some, I slumped forward, holding my head between my knees.

"How did you know?" I mumbled.

"We have been working very hard to put pieces together, evidence, fragments really. Leads are shedding new light, but we have very few voices to testify, to give account to their experiences, very few who survive such...clandestine operations."

I straightened up. "How do you need me to help?"

Laura paused. "First," she reached over the table that had the photographs. "Very simply, I need you to tell me if you can identify some individuals for me...by looking at some photographs."

I inhaled and exhaled laboriously. "Sure." Gaining my feet, I shuffled closer to the designated photograph table.

Laura handed me a black and white. "Do you recognize this person?"

I shook my head. "No."

She plucked it from my hand and replaced it with another picture, one in color. "How about this one?"

"No, I'm afraid not."

"Look at it closely. Are you absolutely sure?"

"I'm sure." Although, I admit, there was something familiar about the individual. I just couldn't put my finger on it.

"All right," Laura flipped through the spread, dispersing them into a wider space. "How about this one?"

I shrugged, tightening my lips with doubt, and grabbed the picture. Then the picture grabbed me. My mouth opened but I couldn't utter anything. I felt a hand squeeze my shoulder.

"Sylvia? Are you okay?"

Finally, I cupped my mouth and sighed through my fingers. "Frick."

"I beg your pardon?"

I cleared my throat. "I called him *Frick*."

"Hm." Laura nodded. "Did this man torture you, Sylvia? Was he involved somehow?"

Words evaded me. Everything went blank, numb. My legs grew unsteady.

Laura and my mom's arms went around my torso in support. "Do you need to sit down?"

"No, no." I pressed a hand against my forehead. "No, I'll be fine."

After a pause, Laura said, "This man, 'Frick' as you call him, well his name is Captain Héctor Nazario, and he is with…"

Laura stopped talking when I grabbed for a particular photo from off the table that screamed at me. This one had the person's name written in thick black felt marker in the white frame underneath it. I stared at it. *Horacio Emilio Botello.* I tested the words on my tongue, whispering it. My eyes floated back to the image captured of the man in army green and loaded to the hilt with weapons and ammo. He looked like a regular Rambo. I knew he had a real name but it was strange to see it in this context, after knowing him as only one thing, my torturer named Puma. His real name and not some moniker made my ordeal with them seem unreal, like it never happened. I shuddered and drew an arm around my own waist. "This is Puma," I said softly, almost with disbelief.

"Puma?" Laura asked. "Puma…hmm." She paused. "His real name is Horacio Emilio Botello…"

I'm not blind.

"Aliases, Donato Burgos, Hernán Ocampo. He is a member of the *Policía Nacional de Colombia*, a lieutenant."

My eyebrows knit together; I could feel my all over frown cloud my comprehension.

Laura nodded and enlightened me. "The National Police of Colombia."

"Police?" I said.

"They are not like the local police force, but a gendarmerie. They operate as a military armed force, part of the Ministry of Defense. Established to bring order, enforce tranquility, and to adjudicate public civil tensions and uprisings between the two primary political parties of Colombia, the liberal and the conservative, their original design was understandable and needed. However, things have a way of shifting under your nose in Colombia, Sylvia, in case you have not noticed."

I glared at her.

"I am sorry, I did not mean to offend you, or demean what has happened to you personally or your understanding of it. Cathi, your mother, told me you are not politically active, nor have interest in things of this nature."

"No. But an interest is growing." I clenched my teeth.

"Good. I was hoping that would be the case." Laura continued, "Lieutenant Botello—and his cohorts," she exhaled with weariness, "are believed to be a part of a rightwing paramilitary group responsible for carrying out a sort of *dirty war* against leftist rebels, guerrillas, any suspected supporters or collaborators. We are not sure, but we think they may be linked with the United Self-Defense Forces of Colombia—in Spanish they are known by the acronym AUC—a so-called organization connecting and consolidating local and regional rightwing extremist paramilitary groups. Their main objectives are to guard the nation's trade and industry interests, as well as combat leftist guerrillas, such as FARC and ELN." Laura rubbed her hands together. "Former Colombian President Álvaro Uribe tried to subdue the aggression by signing a peace pact with AUC. Yet, paramilitary infiltration has shaken the country. Still, there is such aggression." She shuddered. "They continue to violate human rights. The difference lies only in *how* they operate. They have divided into smaller groups, maneuver more clandestinely. However, still they perform their injustice, do their dirty work.

"There was the foreign aid bill in two thousand eight, in which Congress mandated twenty million dollars designated to the office of the prosecutor-general, because Congress admitted weakness in the justice system. Still, sixty-five percent of that was intended for military. I will not die well unless I die taking down military commanders with me."

"Seriously?" I thought Laura came off as scrappy, but she didn't exactly strike me as the fighting type.

"Of course, but I am speaking in a manner of seeking retribution, of prosecution." She forced a slight smile. "Anyway, this dirty war is something you fell into. And it should have never happened—to you, to anybody!"

Laura sat on the lip of the table, folded her hands and asked, "So, tell me...what did they do to you, how did it occur?"

I wasn't sure I wanted to share my story. I wasn't sure I was ready, if I'd ever be ready. But Laura remained strong in her encouragement, unwavering in her support. Once I opened my mouth and the first few words tripped out, the rest came forth like a deluge from a dam that just broke open.

It seemed like an eternity passed when I spoke, and even longer afterward, when Laura assessed my testimony, even jotting notes down, before she gave any sort of response. She rubbed her deep-set eyes, her face, breathed with the weight of a ton of bricks. "I am so sorry for what you have endured," she finally spoke. "I can help you, if you will trust me."

"Help me do what?" I asked.

"To make right what has been done wrong. To seek retribution for these offenses you have endured."

"I'm not sure I understand what you mean. What are you asking? What am I not hearing here?"

"Sylvia," she brought her hands together in front of her chest. "I want you to return with me to Colombia in order to document your testimony before a panel..."

"No way," I shook my head with exaggerated emphasis.

"This trip would be to meet with the official board there, provide details and answer any questions that come up, which you might have answers for that I would have failed to ask. There are key individuals there who wish to speak with you." She crossed her arms. "Then, simply, you go home afterward. When enough evidence is in place, you fly back to Colombia again and bear witness against your perpetrators. Who, may I remind you," she said while straightening her carriage, "we are working feverishly to stop in their murderous, rightwing criminal conspiracy," she spat. "And, finally, we will help put them before the high court to receive the sentences they deserve."

My neck started to strain, I shook my negative response with such vigor.

"We need you, Sylvia. You must return to Colombia to testify against those who have hurt you. If not you, well, then who? Who will do it? You are alive and have a voice."

"I can't," I whispered hoarsely. "Puma said he didn't want to see me in Colombia again. He warned me. If I returned, I'd definitely disappear—forever."

Laura picked Puma's—*Horacio Emilio Botello's*—photograph up, and then Frick's, flapping them in the air as if she tried to make a dog perform a trick. Her jaw clenched and moved as if she chewed a piece of tough, stringy meat. Then she sputtered as if she worked her tongue between her teeth. She reached over and thumbed through a particular stack of photos. "We believe there is a clandestine concentration camp, one of three that we know of, that is like what you have described. In a mountain...in the *Farallones de Cali*, a pipeline that served many rivers, ultimately feeding into the Cauca, and helping to provide water and electricity to the city of Cali...that pipeline, never completed, was closed years ago." Laura sifted through three or four pictures and then handed me one. "Does this area look familiar?"

I shrugged. "Yeah, I guess."

"How about this?"

I stared at the familiar entrance to The Water Cave with a lump in my throat.

"This is your *La Cueva del Agua*, is it not?" Laura's eyebrows lifted.

When I didn't answer, she said, "If you wish to answer, you would become the first to verify this. You are lucky, no?"

I closed my eyes, remembering Lola, feeling as if someone socked the air out of me.

"Will you help us, Sylvia? We need you." Laura tossed the photos down with a flick of her wrist. "How many more lives will be lost, how many will endure what you have endured until someone speaks up against these injustices—how many, hmm?"

"Okay, okay." My breath came out shakily. "I will do what I can to help."

Twenty-three
Vacillation

I went back and forth to Portland from my home in Vancouver to Laura Aguilera's office, and the entire span produced a rather large knot in my stomach. Tension surfaced. I suppose the prospect of returning to Colombia had me on edge, let alone facing Puma...Lieutenant Botello, that is.

Laura sat in the usual metal foldout chair behind the rectangular foldout table, the one full of photographs. She glanced up when she saw me. "Ah, Sylvia, you are here early, good." Laura stood. She ambled around the collection of tables so she stood next to me. "Are you ready to make another statement? Juan Saiz is here and would like to speak with...to hear your testimony, actually."

My shoulders folded forward in a partial collapse. "I've already given it. Can't he listen to the recordings?"

"He has. He has some questions he would like to ask you, though." Laura lifted her chin and stared at me down the length of her nose, examining me. "Do you feel okay, Sylvia? Can I get you some water?"

I held my palms up and then clasped them behind my head, stretching my neck. "No. No water, thanks, and no—I don't feel okay."

"What is the matter, what can I do to ease your trouble?"

I splayed my arms, my hands, in a violently quick motion, "This. All of this is the matter. It's all trouble. I don't want to go back to Colombia—I do not want to face these people…"

"Sylvia, you cannot think of only yourself, but of all the others, those you suffered alongside, those who will endure the same fate, those…"

"No! I am not thinking of myself! I am not," I huffed. "When does it stop, when does it all stop!" I roared. I pushed the table over. Photographs slid and flickered to the floor. "Ugh, what do you want from me…" Cupping my face, I mumbled through my hands, "Oh God, Laura, I am so sorry. I don't know what's happening to me."

After a reign of silence, other than my sniffles, she draped an arm over my shoulders and patted my arm. Then I joined her on the floor to gather the clash of militaristic images.

"Nobody is forcing you, Sylvia. But, we are hopeless if we sit back, idle. As we speak, others are being kidnapped and tortured, their basic rights as human beings violated and stripped. Other women, such as yourself, are going through, right now, what you went through. We are desperate for your assistance. For that, I ask for your forgiveness."

Sitting back on my haunches, I sighed and dropped my arms on my denim-covered thighs with a dull smack. "You don't have to ask for forgiveness, Laura. I understand your position. I can fathom what you are trying to accomplish. But I've told you before—I'm confused and, and...conflicted about testifying against Puma." I witnessed her glare and corrected myself, "I mean Botello."

She nodded with firm approval. "You must do this. When the time comes, and we have gathered all the necessary evidence, you testify against *all* of them that we place in the seats of legal prosecution. At least *they* will get an official trial in a permissible court. That's more than they did for you, when they thought you were guilty of subversion, uh?" She flicked her chin before she scooped up another bunch of candid snapshots.

"Yes," I said, "they deserve repercussions for their actions, but...Puma...is different. He did end up saving my life. I happen to know that he, for a fact, disobeyed orders to do so. I don't want to testify against him. I'm here today because of him."

"And you were *there* because of him also. Do not forget! Horacio Botello is a kidnapper, a torturer and a murderer. I cannot comprehend *what sort of thing* transpired between the two of you, but if you testify against any of them, you must testify against him."

I stood. "Then I won't. And for the record, I don't like the suggestive manner with which you've said '*what sort of thing* transpired...' That's uncalled for."

"Please, wait!" Laura stopped me from walking out. "Forgive me for my anger. I did not mean to take it out on you. Please...let us buy you dinner, Juan and I. We will talk. Please," she asked, the worry in her voice stabbing me with guilt.

After a gazing pause, I nodded with a long sigh and said, "Okay."

I don't know what I expected over lunch. Maybe Laura apologizing over the way she phrased things or the inappropriate conclusions she had drawn. When I explained I didn't want to testify against Botello because, even though he catapulted me into a private hell, he also took great personal risks to get me out of Colombia alive, Laura stared at me with apathy. She didn't get it. Perhaps nobody would—*I* don't know.

When I made it clear what I sensed was a call from God to pray for Puma—and yes, it was difficult to call him anything other than his moniker—Laura rolled her eyes, shook her head with anger, gulped her water, and then proceeded to work on plying me to her will and that of the board. Then, while I spelled out the most prominent reason for my hesitation in returning to Colombia, my fear of the whole thing recurring but with fatal consequences, Laura promised me protection.

They would hire a security service, assured Saiz.

"You have nothing to fear. You will be protected," Laura declared.

"If I go and do what you ask, will you help me find my brother?"

With elbows on the table, Laura leaned on her ring-clad hands. "I do not think you will find your brother, Sylvia." She started twisting and rubbing her fingers.

"Answers to his disappearance then," I sat back with a puff of air forced between my pressed lips.

"Yes," she replied.

"Yes," Juan added.

"Then yes," I said. "When do we leave?"

Twenty-four
Locating Little Ana

A little over two weeks later, I sat on an airplane next to Laura Aguilera—destination Bogotá. Leaving home didn't give me a dose of apprehension; saying goodbye to Mom and Dad did. Mom looked like she'd crack into a zillion pained pieces right before my eyes. "I'll be okay," I assured her, but I don't think she was convinced. I wasn't either.

I don't remember when I fell asleep, but the especially hard bounce that made the plane take air again before it set down to a screeching halt jarred me to consciousness.

"We are here...Bogotá," Laura smiled weakly, her eyes puffy from the onset of jetlag.

Laura kept waiting for me, ushering me along by gently guiding my arm, but I think my legs filled with lead and my head cotton. She must have given up, for I located her way up ahead of me this time. My heart about lunged out of my chest and I trotted to catch up. "Don't leave me," I muttered with thick speech, the effects of long distance travel and exhaustion.

"I know you are tired. At least try to keep up."

"Right. We have a lot to cover in a short amount of time," I reiterated her earlier words.

Forty minutes later, we entered her modest apartment somewhere in the Bosa district of the nation's capital.

Darkness of the night clung to me like the cloak of Count Dracula. I couldn't shake the fatigue. Although Laura insisted we stay up and work through some documents, my yawning perturbed her and so she scooted to the micro kitchen in a hurry to make us some coffee. I'd rather take a bed, but coffee would have to do since no other options came into immediate view. I had to hand it to Laura; the woman knew how to focus with an intensity I've not seen before.

Plopping down into her small sofa, I sipped my cup of dark yet lively brew and rested my head back while Laura thrummed through papers.

Suddenly, she blurted, "Tomorrow we journey to the north of Bogotá."

"Why?"

"When your mother and father were here and we searched for you, as well as your brother, a very frightened individual told us Ana had sought safety and left the city. She is staying with family in another region, the Meta department."

"Ana...?"

"Ana Delarosa de Vélez," Laura said in disbelief. "Your brother's girlfriend...estranged from her spouse...?"

"Ah, yes, Ana. I didn't even know her full name."

"Well, now you do."

"So she's alive? She ought to have some answers." I brightened.

"She is more or less in hiding and," Laura said in a singsong, yet discouraging way, "reluctant to talk. Let us get some sleep."

Gladly, I thought.

I had just fallen asleep when Laura woke me.

"What is it, what's wrong?" I asked.

"Nothing is wrong, unless this hour in which to get out of bed is incorrect," she laughed.

I rubbed the blurriness from my eyes, trying to read the clock. "What time is it?"

"It is already morning. I gather you slept well, out like a light, shall I say?" She started to amble out of the room. "Breakfast is ready. I made *Calentado*. Come and eat it while it is still heated."

I caught her smile before I sat up and got dressed.

Sitting at her small kitchen table, I stared at the plate as she explained the dish to me. *Chorizo*, *arepa*, a side of rice and beans covered in *hogao*, a traditional tomato and onion seasoning sauce, topped with a fried egg. Some of it looked appetizing. Given my daily prison staple, I didn't think I could eat rice and beans again.

The inviting aroma of hot chocolate drifted to my nose. My gaze settled on the mug near me. I lifted the cup and downed half of its creamy contents before I picked up my fork to eat. "Thanks, Laura." I noted the savory flavors of the *hogao* that would make anything taste good. Hungrier than I thought, I ate every bite.

After breakfast, I cleaned up while Laura saw to papers, namely, directions southeast, into the Meta department, whereas Bogotá was situated in the Cundinamarca department. There, we hoped to find Spencer's girlfriend, Ana, through whom we wished to learn of Spencer's whereabouts. A slight optimistic pang dared throb in my chest that maybe, just maybe, Spencer resided there with Ana, and that they were in hiding together.

We drove to the far side of the capital city, kept driving away from Bogotá to beyond. We drove over bridges, through tunnels. The mountains often consumed the view. At some point, somewhere in one of the valleys of the eastern mountainous outskirts, the roads had become potholed, dirt paths in which Laura maneuvered her small, compact car. A ranch came into view far in the distance. Laura stopped the car and killed the engine.

"*La estancia,*" she pointed with her chin. "We go there."

I studied the hilly backdrop, vibrant and green. In its natural beauty, it resonated tranquility; at the same time, the wilds mystified with a silent omen of unruliness. The estate-like compound that rested at its feet gave no less than its surroundings' opposite faces, tranquil and unruly.

"It's quite a ways up there," I said. "Can't we drive?"

"No."

"Why not?"

"Those are the rules." Her driver's door squeaked open.

"What rules?" I met the slam of economized metal.

I caught up with Laura. We trekked through dirt and sometimes mud, just as I wished I had worn hiking boots instead of white sneakers.

The quiet maddened me. When I tried to speak, Laura silenced me. The firmness set in her jaw was bothersome. I started fidgeting with my sweatshirt, my sleeves, my hair, rubbing an eternal itch on the tip of my nose.

I about jumped out of my shoes when I noticed two weapon-wielding men and a woman dressed in cammies following close behind. They formed a perfect soundless triangle.

Closing my eyes, I breathed, or tried to, but panic started to set in. "What is the military doing…doing, what are they doing here? Why are *we* here?" My whisper came out hoarse, frantic.

Laura whispered back. "Relax. These are members of FARC that I told you, Revolutionary Armed Forces of Colombia. They are anti-military…well, against the right wing, anyway."

When she said that, I noticed the uniforms they donned varied. In fact, one wore a regular tee-shirt with some rock band's name printed on it under an army green jacket, and camouflage pants.

"*You* don't look relaxed," I accused her. The threat grew when two more members materialized out of the woodwork and flanked us. I glanced over my shoulder. At some point, two more stealthily brought up the rear. It was a regular guerrilla train. I wanted to yell, Choo! Choo! but I didn't like the direction this train was going.

"This is considered the Eastern Bloc of FARC. We are in their territory."

"That's not reassuring." I moved so close to Laura as we whispered our dialogue, that I bumped her and made her stumble.

She glared at me as she righted herself. "I have been here before, and if we stay calm, they will follow us all the way to the *estancia* where we can speak to my contact person."

"Ana?"

"No. But Ana is there."

I grabbed Laura's arm, slowing her. "I thought you said she was hiding—with family." I rasped.

"This is her family."

"You're kidding me, right? Ana is a guerrilla?"

Laura stopped. I froze. The counterparts carrying weapons reacted on cue, as if quicker than our own shadows.

"I knew I should have explained this before we left, but I did not think you would come if I had."

I raised my brows. "You're right."

Laura thinned her lips. "We are here now. Let us move forward and take care of our business."

After about thirty seconds, I jogged to catch up to Laura. Especially when I realized we each had train cars assigned to us, and nobody likes a disassembled train, particularly me.

La estancia consisted of one main building with a cluster of smaller structures surrounding it. I noticed tents pitched even farther out, near a creek. When we approached a high wall with a wooden door, the door opened flimsily and out stepped a salt and peppered-bearded man wearing sunglasses and a green cap. An unlit cigarette butt dangled from the corner of his mouth.

"Laura," he exclaimed, as he grabbed her with hearty fervor and kissed her.

"You are still trying to quit, uh?"

"*Sí…*" The man made a sound of disgust while flicking the cigarette butt to the ground. "It will kill me before one of the lizards does."

Laura laughed and turned toward me. She marked my wide eyes, reassuring me I did not have to worry about poisonous lizards around *la estancia*. "Vasco here calls members of a particular paramilitary group *Los Lagartos*, The Lizards. Botello and Nazario are lizards. That might interest you," she said in a joking manner.

I smirked, not in a particularly friendly way. To be honest, I didn't think it was that cute at all. Besides, I could barely keep up with all these nicknames and aliases. The line between reality and make-believe blurred, making it difficult to know what was what and who was who.

Vasco patted me on the back, and with a wide smile welcomed me into the enlarged courtyard, the size of a corral, only with a ten-foot, cement privacy wall around it. Inside, many people milled about. Some sat playing cards, some cooked over open fire, some napped under the sun, and others studied maps and documents spread across a table.

"Are you hungry, can I have someone get you something?" Vasco kindly asked.

I shook my head.

"A drink then, you must be thirsty...coffee, beer, *aguardiente*?"

I recalled my brother favoring *aguardiente*, or *burning water*, as he explained to me, a high content alcoholic drink made from sugar cane and flavored with aniseed. Greatly disliking the taste of licorice, aside from the fact I've never been in the habit of drinking alcohol, I shook my head.

He leaned back and examined me with disappointment. "Ah, well, you will change your mind," he decided.

"Come, sit, my friends." Vasco gestured to an already occupied table. One suggestive glance by the commander in a cap and the comfortably seated threesome vacated their seats and moved elsewhere.

We sat and stared at each other. I started fidgeting again. A moment later, I noticed a pair of sandaled feet standing next to me. I glanced up.

"Ana." I recognized her immediately.

She gave one resolute nod.

"Vasco and I have some catching up to do." Laura said, as she stood with him. "And I think you two do as well."

In the seat opposite me, Ana lowered herself as if she weighed lighter than a feather. She kept her head poised a certain way...proud, maybe; a little scared also.

Time passed between us. I didn't know what to say first. If Spencer accompanied her, he would have shown himself. I had a terrible pit to fill in my stomach.

"I loved Spencer," she said.

The pit widened.

"Loved," I said to Ana. "As in, you fell out of love with him, or as in he no longer exists?"

"When I went home one morning, I found the house raided. Spencer did not show up for work. I came here right away, but I sent people to inquire. I know in my heart," she closed her eyes, "that he is dead. The lizards killed him." Her eyelids fluttered open and with pools forming in her eyes, she pleaded sympathy from me by her gaze.

I looked away. I didn't want to have a comfort fest with her.

"Don't you at all feel responsible for his disappearance?" I faced her again.

Ana's posture grew defiant. "What do you mean?"

I wanted to see her crumble. "Spencer was no guerrilla, yet you are. He was just a language teacher, for crying out loud!"

She snorted, and then stood. "You have no idea." She turned.

"Wait!" I cried in desperation.

Ana froze. She twisted around, granting me another moment.

"He was my brother. I miss him," I entreated, needing answers to what I didn't know how to ask. "You know they tortured me?"

Ana nodded, and then she came to me and crumbled in my arms while I did in hers. "I am sorry," she cried softly.

The afternoon progressed and I had the feeling I'd come away with little more than when I arrived. Laura was right about Ana; she was hesitant to talk. I wondered about Spencer's involvement with her, and what it actually entailed, but I found denial erecting a wall of defense in my heart. My earlier formulated idea that Ana's estranged yet controlling husband carried out personal retribution against Spencer now struck me as absurd. I also wondered about Ana's five children, but she grew particularly stoic over them. They were elsewhere, in good, safe hands, she said as more of a reassurance to herself.

Ana had earlier slipped into one of the small clapboard buildings. I didn't see her again.

I ambled around the humongous, yet somewhat shanty, courtyard—a courtyard that had once hailed grandeur—ignored. When Vasco and Laura joined me, they were laughing. I wished they'd stop. I misunderstood this excursion, because I thought we journeyed there in a search for answers, but my companion(s) only hosted a party between them.

At last, we sat down together, the three of us. A woman, probably someone's mother who dedicated herself to her grown child's cause, placed bowls of food in front of us and a plate of *arepas*. I glanced at the food and then at the chickens clucking freely around the premises. Well, one of them didn't make it.

"What is this place, the Revolutionary's home base or something?"

Vasco chewed and swallowed. "No. Our fronts sometimes need to congregate, to strengthen our coalition, to discuss and reaffirm objectives."

"Fronts?" I asked.

"*Sí*," Vasco said. "We have numerous units, many factions that carry out various activities, you might say. Divided into different groups, covering the regions, but we all have the same cause." He thumped his chest. "I am a part of the Eastern Bloc. Although many of us like to now—well, since two thousand ten, September—refer to the Eastern Bloc as *Bloque Comandante Jorge Briceño* in honor of one of our leaders who was killed." He leaned back. "Our faction is considered to be one of the strongest of our people's army," Vasco said proudly. "We control the eastern and central-eastern territory of Colombia."

"What do you mean by 'control'?"

Vasco eyed me sharply, yet he had a slight air of amusement. "We do what we must to advance our political, philosophical, and..." he shrugged, "financial goals."

I glanced around. Many people mingled about, but the compound itself, although large and more than adequate to accommodate the numbers, appeared rundown.

Vasco seemed to catch my drift. He smiled.

"This place, these grounds serve our purpose." He gave an inside look Laura's way. "I should invite you to my house one day." He slipped his hand from Laura's, a gesture I didn't even notice until that moment, and selected a semi-burnt *arepa* from the plate near her arm.

A cool wind had whipped over the floor of the mountains' feet as the sun began dipping. Loose dirt silt in the courtyard rose in the air. I stared at my mostly untouched unlucky chicken. I thought of Spencer. Had Ana brought him here at one time? If so, what ran through his mind as he began understanding the woman whom he loved was and with what she affiliated herself?

"What is Ana's part in all this?" I asked softly.

"Ah," Vasco said with pride. "Ana is a good rebel."

I looked at him suspiciously. She didn't strike me as a rebel in the first place.

"She handles much of the organizational aspects of the *Teófilo Forero* Front."

"Huh?" My face contorted with incomprehension.

Laura said, "Also known as the Fifty-fifth Front."

Vasco bowed his head admirably toward her with a glint in his eye.

Oh brother, I thought.

He turned his attention back to me. "FARC's base in Bogotá. Urban militia. Members of the Fifty-fifth operate, conduct activity, in the capital, around it." He shrugged.

"What does 'operate' and 'conduct activity' mean? What do you do?"

"Anything we must to suppress and annihilate those who suppress and annihilate us. In one region it might mean a taxation issue, economic, or agricultural..."

"Illegal drug trade?" I said sarcastically. "Monopolizing Colombia's moneymaking fields to build your empire?"

"May I remind you, *Señora*, you are in *my* country."

Adequately warned, I closed my mouth. I knew what punishment tasted like.

"In another region," he continued, "our focus might be on politicians who oppose us, who try to wipe us out by giving power to rightwing forces that work to reduce our numbers."

"Why can't you work to get along?"

Vasco laughed. "Because conservatism is poison to our souls. It holds people back from progress, from necessary change. And capitalism corrupts."

"I'm sure conservative thinkers would say the same about liberal ideology. And capitalists would call socialism the great leveler which stifles ambition and personal growth by taking and distributing wealth. For small business owners, that could create a lot of problems, douse a lot of hopes to succeed and do well."

With a wry grin, he said, "Spoken by a true capitalist."

I doubted he intended that as a compliment.

"Sylvia," he addressed me pointedly. "I wish very much for us to be great friends. I will bring down the lizards who did the unspeakable. I will help you get justice for what they did...to you, to your brother. A vengeful revolutionary is a force to reckon with."

I clamped my open mouth shut, only to revive it with a bang. "I thought I came back to Colombia to give my testimony." I glanced at Laura, then back to Vasco. "I'm not looking for a hit man." I turned abruptly to Laura. "Is this your 'security service'?"

Vasco started to rub his beard. "You need our assistance," he tried to convince me over a strangely quiet Laura. "And we need yours. Now," he leaned forward, "if you will, tell me every detail of your capture."

I huffed and worked the kinks out of my neck. "It's difficult to keep going over this!"

"This is understandable," said Vasco.

"Laura has the recordings and documentation." I spread my hands in frustration. "I want to go home, back to Laura's, I mean. I'm tired."

Laura said, "We're sleeping here tonight."

"Seriously?"

"Okay, okay," Vasco lifted his hands in compliance. "I have memorized your testimony. I will only ask you questions. You would only have to answer them. What do you say, uh?"

Questions make me scream.

"Sure, why not?" I retorted.

During more of a friendly-turning discussion, I supplied everything I knew. As I ended up reliving the horror, a large part of me wanted to see the guerrillas unleash their vengeance on those who messed me up, those who robbed me of a part of my identity, my life. Then an undertone niggled, an omen hinted that I wasn't seeing the entire puzzle. Pieces were missing. I just didn't know what. Being back in Colombia made me nervous. I suppose making a connection with the guerrillas should make me feel safe, protected, but those feelings, overall, evaded me a while back.

I went through the whole thing again. At some point, we moved inside the main building, an old large house converted into separate workstations and sleeping quarters, into a dimly lit room. Once, when giving my testimony, Laura backed me up.

She wanted to know exactly where, from The Water Cave, the unmarked grave was, where Puma and I buried Lola. I tried to recall everything about that incident, but I found it difficult to sort through. I pondered the notion that my subconscious buried the episode as I tried to bury the images of Lola's broken, lifeless body.

Laura scribbled notes on a pad.

We went late into the night. To the best of my ability, I answered Vasco's questions. I think I was beginning to trust him, too.

Laura led me to a room partitioned by a curtain. There was a mat on the floor. "You will sleep here, okay? I assure you, you will be safe."

Bringing my eyes from the mat, I looked at her. "Where are you going to sleep?"

She swayed her shoulders some, and uttered something in a singsong way, not really answering. Her mischievous grin said it all.

I watched her back disappear. She ran to her lover's arms, no doubt.

The mat was *completely* unnecessary, I thought, grumbling, as I fell back. I could feel every inch of the concrete floor. Shaking my head, I mumbled, "What have I gotten myself involved in?"

Twenty-five
The Old Church

Late the next morning, I found myself sitting on the sofa at Laura's small place in the capital city. She hummed as she busied herself with paperwork.

"You didn't tell me you and Vasco were such an item," I said.

She grinned. "Ah, well, we are a couple who is part-time. On and off, you know. Yesterday, today, we happen to be on." Laura grabbed her digital recorder.

"How about marriage, would you consider it?"

After a hearty exclamation, Laura assured me Vasco had no interest in commitment.

I lowered my chin.

"You will need to prepare to give your testimony in front of the board. Twelve will be on the panel who will hear what you have to say tomorrow. It will be recorded, and then afterward they will question you."

My head came up. "Will you be there?"

"Yes, of course." She shuffled some papers, gathering them up in a bundle and shoving them into a satchel. "Right now, I have to go to the office. You can stay here. Rest," Laura suggested. "It should be fairly quiet."

"Laura?"

"*Sí?*" She stopped with her hand resting on the doorknob.

"What happens after I meet with the panel?"

"Then you can go home, like I have said before, until we call you back. And that will occur after we can present enough evidence to bring your perpetrators to the high court. At that time, you will testify as a part of their trial." She opened the door and paused, bright sunlight washing out her frame. I squinted. "Oh, there will be two anthropologists present, one in forensics, who are most interested in Lola's unmarked grave. I wanted to warn you, so that you are best prepared to provide every detail. It might be a good thing to do this afternoon, recall as much as you can about the event, location, descriptions, etcetera."

I nodded.

"See you in the evening sometime. I will bring us dinner." Laura shut the door.

Slouching back in the couch, I sighed and rubbed my face. First thing I wanted to do was take a shower. Maybe it would do more than cleanse and refresh me. Maybe it would wash my nerves down the drain as well.

After an hour of burning a path across Laura's living room floor by my pacing, I couldn't stand it anymore. Even after attempts at focusing, every time I conjured Lola up in my mind, I had the overwhelming urge to open a closet door and sink down into the darkness, in my self-made cell, closing the door to the rest of the world.

I didn't want to be alone. Occasional bumps and noises from adjoining apartments terrified me. I wrung my hands until they glowed red. Practiced breathing...in...out, in...out, proved worthless. Laura's cell phone number flashed in my mind. I concentrated on the digits I could see in my mind's eye. I grappled with the idea of calling her, because I didn't want to bother her, encumber her with my panic attack. Desperation ate at me, but I didn't call.

Someone came to mind, the only other person I knew in Bogotá who lingered in my mind since talk of returning happened. I couldn't think of anything else to remedy the anxieties that assailed me except face the real issues that haunted me. With an ounce of pretended courage, I walked into the light of day after hailing a taxi service.

Not long after, I traipsed into his office.

"You shouldn't be here," he said. The words stung.

I studied the ugly yellow area rug, my hands limp in my lap.

"Mr. Goren," I said. "I know you know more than you're letting on. Please, anything you can tell me…"

"You're wasting your time…"

I sobbed, whispering weakly, "Please…"

Chuck Goren muttered an oath. He collapsed into his brass studded and leather wingback chair. "Spencer Abbot, your brother, had ties with…"

"Mr. Goren?" His secretary's voice came over the loudspeaker.

He stretched to press a button. "What is it now?"

"Your two o'clock has arrived."

"All right," he remarked with a snip and stood. "FARC."

I gaped at him, "Excuse me?" *I hate cussing.*

He leaned backward with his hands on his lower back, stretching. "Revolutionary Armed Forces of Colombia." He winced. "The People's Army," he said sardonically.

"In Spanish, *Fuerzas Armadas Revolucionarias de Colombia*—otherwise known as, FARC."

"Oh."

"And now, Ms. Abbott, I really cannot and should not help you, so if you'll excuse me, I have an appointment with someone who actually called ahead to schedule one."

"So if I called first I'd get an appointment?"

"No." He transferred some papers into a file, slid it into a briefcase and closed it.

I considered the option of crying. That unnerved men more than anything.

"I see." I chewed on the inside of my cheek, almost biting through the tissue. "Would it change your mind to know I have provided my testimony for the Human Rights Retributive Board of Colombia, and that they are preparing to bring Lieutenant Horacio Botello, among others, to trial?" I sat forward and spread my fingers on the edge of his wide mahogany desk.

He froze, and then started moving again as if on slow defrost setting.

"Yeah," I sat back and wove my fingers together in a scholarly fashion. "I didn't feel the need to mention you, but I just may change my mind." I twirled all the way around once in the swivel chair.

He moved to the other side of the office and poured himself a drink. I heard his gulp and half-coughed sigh. "Why are you doing this?"

I stood. "I just want to know the truth about my brother. That's all."

"I can't tell you what you want to know. I simply do not have that information. He was linked to FARC." Goren shrugged with indifference.

"Even I know that...now." I gazed out the window, seeing nothing. "You must have more knowledge of this..."

"I don't," Mr. Goren scolded me. "Now, I have an appointment." He raised his brows.

"Oh, I'm dismissed am I? Well, then the retributive board will have an especially interesting day tomorrow. They'll not only be shocked but very interested to hear your inclusion in the unlawful practices against me."

"I had nothing to do with it. I didn't touch you." he scowled and slammed down his glass.

Zooming closer to the man, I challenged him. "You're right. You didn't, but you...you're linked with who did, like my brother had been linked, as you say, with FARC." I snorted and nodded my head. "He had an inopportune girlfriend he blubbered over. That was his only fault."

Chuck Goren gazed at me. "Don't involve me," he said, quietly. "I don't want to be involved."

"You don't have to be," I assured him. "I don't want to ruin your reputation, your life."

"Then, what...what do you want from me?"

"Tell me where I can find Lieutenant Horacio Botello. That's all. I know you know him. I know he prearranged to drop me off at the embassy that day when I walked straight off a killing field into your office." I swallowed against the lump in my throat. "I just want to talk to him, and I won't involve you. I won't bother you again if you just tell me where I can find him."

He ambled back to the desk and slumped into his leather wingback. "He's on leave. He won't want to be bothered."

I cocked my head in a challenge. "You're pretty good friends, then, aren't you?"

"Not after today," he sighed. "*Agua de Dios.*"

"Pardon me?"

"Botello lives in *Agua de Dios.*" Chuck scribbled an address down on a piece of paper, ripped it off the tablet and then extended it, head down, without looking at me. "It's southwest from here about a hundred and fourteen kilometers, that's just over seventy-one miles. Take a bus, van, whatever. There are several reliable transport services. Should take about an hour, maybe two, to get there." He loosened his tie and stretched his collar. "Call a cab company and reserve a taxi. You'd probably feel safer."

"Concerned for my safety, are you?" I snatched the address from him.

He pressed his lips into a thin line. "I've given you what you want. Will you keep your word and leave me out of all this?"

I nodded, "Yeah. Thanks," I said softly and left.

Three and a half hours later, my taxi rolled into the small town of *Agua de Dios*. I didn't care how much it cost. Goren was right; I wanted to feel safe.

I desired to speak with Puma without Laura's knowledge. Battling fear, yet constantly pushing it aside, this became my own mission, my true reason for coming back to Colombia in the first place. I just didn't realize it until I saw Spencer's girlfriend, Ana, yesterday. My brother's absence ate at me. Like a giant question mark, it stabbed me day after day—where are you—what happened to you—how did you leave us—why? It haunted me. How can one bury the dead when there is no body to bury? There's no closure.

Now I wandered down a quiet street of a strange town, passing an old stone church. Down a ways from the house of worship and on the opposite side of the road sat the house I sought. I moved closer to it. When I compared the address from the one jotted on the piece of paper to the one I stood in front of, my breathing transitioned to shaking gasps. Proceeding through the narrow breezeway to the sea green front door, I paused and then I knocked.

No answer.

I stood there a while. At last, I sat on the single cement step and studied the stone walkway. It appeared homespun, yet there was beauty in its simplicity.

Not knowing how much time had passed, I figured I needed to get up and do something. I moseyed around the premises and peeked in a window, the only window I could get near due to all the growth. It was cultivated growth...flowers, a garden, a little courtyard...all very simple, maintained and quaint.

The thought occurred to me that Puma might linger inside, well aware of my presence, but I didn't have that sense. The serenity and the quietness about put me to sleep. I almost chuckled at the contrast of my torturer's home to the torturer's chamber.

I walked again.

Agua de Dios. Water of God. Not to mention the town also hailed the nickname, City of Hope. The irony killed me. I boiled in the pits of hell at The Water Cave, and now I waded through the Water of God, roaming the streets of the City of Hope. Did that mean God would give me a revelation here? Would he cleanse me, with one final sweep, from all hatred, bitterness, and depression—every trace?

Yeah, I prayed to forgive my enemy.

But I still wanted answers—for Spencer, for my mom and dad.

I came to the old stone church again. It reeked of history and staunch holiness. Surprised to find the door unlocked, I stepped inside with barely a sound. Candles burned. Paintings of Jesus, and of his mother, Mary, commanded my attention.

Crossing through the vestibule, I entered the sanctuary. Dimly lit, it was empty. I sauntered toward the altar, passing rudimentary wooden pews. The stained glass of angels ministering to Jesus, ushering him upward to heaven, hung in the back center, beyond the pulpit and a large gold cross took precedence at the foot of it.

A dark shape in my periphery caught my eye. My vision drifted to the left. That's when I noticed a person slumped over a very low altar rail, as if the individual were desperate to obtain access into the holy of holies. It appeared to be a man. He didn't move. In fact, he looked dead. I would know. However, I knew he wasn't. Yet, the way his body sprawled struck me as pained, desperate. I would know that, too. My heart wrenched, yet I couldn't seem to pull away. I didn't want to intrude on his private meeting with God but I longed to watch him. It ministered to me, and so I prayed for him within my mind after I tiptoed to the first pew and sat down. My eyes roamed from the man to the cross and stained glass to the back of him.

Then his back raised and he released a horrible sob as if someone just forced breath into his lungs against his will. I couldn't take the spectacle anymore. I knew it wasn't my business and I should just leave the man to his own private sorrow, but I approached him and sat on the step near him.

"*Perdón?*" I asked quietly. "*Perdón,*" I said again.

The man froze.

"Is there...is there anything I can do to help you?" I leaned closer. The church's acoustics sounded like a vacuum with the tiniest amount of sound falling away. "Can I pray...?"

As if in slow motion, the man rose heavily. He wouldn't face me, but I saw his profile.

I suppose I should have gasped, screamed, cried. I should have known. It was like some cruel trick. In *Agua de Dios* in a little old forsaken church, my torturer laid crumpled across the altar, and now he faced me with tears streaking his cheeks.

Puma. I had to remember him by his own birth name, but oh, he would always be Puma to me. He wearily reached the first pew and sat in it with the heaviness of a burlap sack full of bricks.

Jump on him—that's what I wanted to do—and pound him with my fists. Yet, insanely, I also wanted to comfort his sorrows. God asked me to pray for my enemies, and I did. I needed to see Horacio and sought him out. But I didn't expect to see his brokenness laid bare at the cross, at the feet of Jesus whom the angels were lifting up to heaven. My eyes were not ready for this mental picture in the flesh.

Witnessing his moment of pain, his torrent of anguish, I shivered and wrapped my arms around my girth as I neared the pew and sat next to Horacio. Strange, but I found comfort in the familiar smell of his skin.

We both stared at the scene in the stained glass above the gold cross. An eternity could have passed. We would not have realized. I think part of it did.

Natural light diminished and the church darkened, save for the candles, which burned very low now.

"My brother is dead, isn't he?" I whispered.

I didn't even glance at him, yet I detected the faint nod of his head in my periphery.

He rose and slowly exited the church, casting an occasional gaze in my direction as if beckoning me to follow him...or warning me not to. Confusion settled into my mind.

Ten paces behind him I lingered, but I paused when he started to enter the breezeway of his house.

"I-I have to find a way back to Bogotá. Someone there is expecting me," I said.

"You do not have a ride?" Puma's voice remained low, burdened, as he spoke over his shoulder.

I shook my head, although the darkness probably hid the gesture. "I'll get a taxi."

"I will drive you."

Before I could object, he retraced his steps, walking right past me and back toward the street. Of course, I should have noticed his white car earlier, parked down the side of the quiet road.

We spent the entire drive in silence, much like the only other time I rode in Puma's car. Grateful I remembered Laura's address, partly at the applause of my parents who taught me the skill of memorization, we arrived. Puma killed the engine.

"You're not planning on staying, are you?" I turned to him, surprised.

He drew a hand over his face. "No."

Yet he just sat there.

"Puma…"

"Horacio, please," he said earnestly. "You must call me Horacio. That is my name."

I snorted. "I know you as Puma."

He extended his hand tentatively. "May we start over, as friends… *please?*"

His hand trembled a bit. I didn't think I wanted to accept it, yet I slipped my hand in his. He held my hand gently, warmly and then he released it.

"I'm supposed to testify against you. First, before a panel, and then…"

"I know," he said sadly in the darkness, lit only by a few city lights.

"How would you know this?"

He sucked a breath of air in through his teeth. "That would be the only reason someone in your position would return. Besides," he pointed to the building. "Laura Aguilera lives here."

Now I know my eyes grew large. "You know of Laura?"

"*Sí.* The Human Rights Retributive Board of Colombia will be heard. They will make sure we listen, everybody listens, and Aguilera will lead the commission singlehandedly if she has to. She is the kind of woman who gets her way at whatever cost." Puma pressed back against his seat and rubbed his eyes. "I would like to wash my hands of it all…" his voice drifted to an almost inaudible whisper, "but I cannot… I cannot."

The lights of a passing car flashed through the cabin. I studied Puma's face. "You're wrong, you know."

He questioned me with his gaze.

"Testifying against you isn't why I came back."

Puma turned toward me. "Then why?"

"I really don't want to testify. I don't want to relive it anymore. I don't want to tell the same horrible story again and again." I leaned toward him. "I just need to know. I want to know what happened to my brother, and why this happened to me. I want the truth." My throat constricted, but I held loose emotions intact.

He shook his head in disbelief. "I cannot believe it came to this, and that you and I, here we are, sitting in my car together having *this* conversation." Puma splayed his hands and shook his head again. "If I tell you..."

"You're already in trouble. There's nothing left to risk."

"Sylvia." The way he addressed me made me want to sit up straight. "I will tell you." He sniffed, "Because you deserve to know."

I thought I could hear an antique clock ticking away the minutes, but it was my own heartbeat.

"Your brother was a terrorist."

I gaped at him. That's before I fell into a fit of hysteria. I had to hand it to Puma; he sat there and tolerated my outburst until I had my fill.

"Yeah, right," I finally said, rolling my eyes. "My brother was a language teacher and a nerd. He doesn't..." I cleared my throat. "He didn't have a violent bone in his body."

"You do not believe me?"

"He fell madly in love with a woman who has ties with the Revolutionary Armed Forces of Colombia. That's all."

"No," Puma shook his head with vigor. "No, he was much more than a man who fell in love with one who has *ties,* as you say." I witnessed fury that rose from deep within him, yet he kept it at bay.

"I refuse to believe it."

"You came here for the truth, uh?" he challenged. "But you failed to prepare yourself for the truth. Your mind, your heart, your spirit—what do they tell you?"

"That's not fair. You altered those."

"You are Sylvia Abbott, alive. You are still whole."

"No! You broke me and you know it."

He cringed.

"I will never be the same…"

"Aye, aye aye," he clamped his hands over his head and tugged his hair. "No more, no more…" he reached over and, in a tender manner, touched his fingers against my mouth, sort of patting them, as a mom would do over her child who got a scrape. "Please," he shook his head, begging, and then slipping his hands, gently, softly, almost imperceptibly, he cupped my face in an unexpected display of affection. "I prayed for you. I have prayed every day, every hour…"

"What?" His breath was sweet. My brows furrowed.

He released me and sat back, blowing an unsteady stream of air from his lungs. "I will come back tomorrow, and I will prove to you the truth about your brother."

"What about the retributive board, the panel?"

"Do what you must. What has been done is done, but I will keep my promise to you. When will you be free?"

"Do we have to go anywhere?"

"That depends on you."

A sudden pang of fear hit me. Maybe he intended to make me disappear again, to silence me forever. That would be much simpler for him than facing some of the potential legalities in his future, at least the ones involving me.

"In the name of Jesus, whom I believe in, and whom I know has called me... I give you my promise, you will be safe."

He read my mind... *and*, my torturer, he believed in Jesus. I snorted under my breath. *Great.* I questioned my own faith by Puma's example. How could he possibly be a Christian? If Lieutenant Botello possessed Biblical faith, I wonder if Jesus is really who he says he is. And if so, then what, exactly, possesses me?

Now I *had* to go with him. I had to know.

Twenty-six
Confrontation

That night, after I ran up the stairs to Laura's apartment, closing her door to the outside world, she grilled me with her own set of inquiries. No easier to answer than on the *real* grill at The Water Cave, I stumbled on Laura's version until the truth tripped out of me, at last.

"I'm not going to give my testimony before the panel tomorrow."

She stared at me, blinking.

"Not until I find what I seek. I need to know about my brother, my own circumstance. I need to know what God wants from me, because if Puma is a Christian, I want to know how this is possible...and why."

"Fine," she said. "Do what you feel you must do, but testify first, so the board can hear your story and ask the questions they wish to ask you. Then do what you find is necessary."

"You have a digital recording of my story. Use that..."

"They want to hear it again, but from you personally. They want to be able to ask you in their own examination. You want to simplify everything, but it's much more complicated to build a case against somebody, to gather evidence, and here, you are cavorting with one of the very people we want to bring to justice. Botello is *still* poisoning your mind."

I slapped her.

And then tears slipped down my face. I gazed at her stricken expression through new pools of residual pain. "I'm...I'm sorry," I whispered.

"You have used me, Ms. Abbott." Laura's firm jaw set me off balance.

"No." I could see my hair, my bangs quivering, but I couldn't stop shaking. "No, I didn't use you. I didn't really know why I came back to Colombia until... well, I don't know, but it wasn't to face the retributive board. I know that now."

Laura turned from me.

"Maybe we can reschedule," I offered, "but I have to do this for *me*. In a sense, I feel compelled to face Puma tomorrow. Maybe I'll get the truth."

Laura huffed and spun around. "The truth? Lieutenant Botello, Captain Nazario, all the rest of those lizards are kidnapping innocent individuals, maiming and killing them. You are lucky you survived."

"*Why* do you think I survived?"

"To give the missing persons a voice! To stop human rights abuses, to end violence," she threw her hands into the air. "Violence is unacceptable in any form, and I think, Sylvia, I think you are a hypocrite!"

"A hypocrite. *Really*? No offense, Laura, but isn't cavorting with a commander of a Marxist-Leninist guerrilla group who exercises using violence of historical measures a *tad* hypocritical?"

"Leave my relationship with Vasco out of this!"

"It's not the *relationship* I'm referring to. The blame you've put on me seems the same." I put my fists on my hips. "I am going tomorrow. You can't stop me. Reschedule with the board if you want, but I'm doing this."

"You are acting the fool."

I turned toward her on my way to the bedroom. "Should I get a hotel tonight?"

After a long pause, she finally said, "No. You are still welcome to stay."

"Thank you," I muttered, guilt threatening to disintegrate my demeanor.

"I think I will call Vasco and ask him to send somebody to follow you, to watch and make sure you don't disappear."

"The handy hired security service, huh?" I scratched my temple. "Don't you think Puma would be aware of it? Then he may hurt me after all."

Laura grinned. "You are an idiot to think he is not going to, in the first place."

"You know, I could do without the name-calling."

"And I could do without the slapping."

I stuttered. "I'm really, truly sorry, Laura. I wish I could take it back."

"*Buenas noches*, Sylvia," she said to me before she retracted into her room and shut the door.

I tossed and turned all night, finally getting up and staring out the window at the street scene below, until gray light spread across the buildings and cars. For some reason, I had a sense that things would be different after today.

Laura, an early riser, had gotten up. I heard her shuffle around the apartment for a few minutes and then she exited through the front door. The vibrations of her heavy footfall down the staircase met me like a hammer against my head. I watched her jog down the street, ignoring the dark gray car holding two passengers that had arrived and perched about three hours ago.

Later in the morning, I watched Puma's white car claim a spot up the street. He sat and waited. I wondered if he realized he had entered a showdown, facing the dark gray car a few yards away, compliments of Vasco, a sworn enemy.

Hungry, I grabbed a store-bought sweet roll Laura had left out on the kitchen counter. After drizzling honey on it, I locked up Laura's apartment.

Puma opened the door for me from the inside. He eyed me disapprovingly as I tried to lick beads of honey before it trailed onto the seat of his car.

I devoured half of the roll when I began wondering if I should tell Puma the dark gray car following at an inconspicuous distance behind us had a couple of leftist guerrillas in it sent for my protection. And just as I considered mentioning it, his car suddenly shifted violently.

Tires squealed. I slammed into him. My sticky roll flew out of my hands and stuck to the driver's side window. The same window out of which I glimpsed an outline of a man's dumbstruck face—the driver of the gray car.

As the smell of burnt rubber stung my nose, I realized we had done a one eighty in the middle of a city street and passed my so-called bodyguards...er...security service. I wondered if I should have waved to them.

Just as I climbed back into my seat, the car skidded, making a sharp turn. It fishtailed until it straightened out. Another turn found me yet again in Puma's lap.

Unexpectedly (not that I expected the other events), the car turned sharply again, again fishtailing, but this time I hugged the passenger side door.

"Geez, Puma! Don't you have seatbelts in this thing?"

He answered with nonchalance, "The seatbelt...it is broken. I thought you would have remembered from last night."

"You could have warned me," I scolded.

Puma made a look of disgust as he peeled my sweet roll off the window and gave it a toss outside. He stirred his fingers together, trying to wipe the sticky off. "You should eat better food."

I gaped at him. *He's kidding me, right?*

"It looks like we are alone."

Was that remark really supposed to make me feel at ease? Yet, somehow, his lack of remarking unsettled me. *Um, yeah, we just experienced a mini car chase and he doesn't even ask questions.* I studied his profile and decided to let it go, because apparently he did too.

We drove for hours. I thought we journeyed to *Agua de Dios*, but when we passed the sign, long ago, anxiety niggled even more.

Then we ventured off road, and off road travel in a small car made my stomach lurch, partly because I didn't get the chance to finish breakfast and partly because fear crept up my spine and settled in my digestive tract where it liked to manifest itself. I managed to ask Puma once where he was taking me, but he proved a quiet, private man. Too quiet. Too private.

A field in the middle of nowhere, surrounded by woods—

Laura was right.

Oh, God...forgive me...a fool and idiot.

Puma got out. He lingered, waiting.

I froze. Even if I tried, I couldn't budge.

The car shifted and I glanced up. Puma had placed his hands heavily on the car hood and stared at me through the windshield, impatience wearing thin on his expression. He mouthed, "Trust me."

Yeah, right. I still didn't move.

He clasped his hands in the form of a prayer and pleaded with me.

My hands drifted to the car handle. I attempted to open it, but strength slipped from me. I tried again, this time (darn hands) the door opened. I stepped out only to collapse to my knees.

Puma brought me to my feet and I leaned against him.

After a few fleeting moments, he spoke softly in my ear, "Your brother rests here."

I sobbed then, nearly suffocating. Then I pummeled Puma with my fists. He took the beating, and then held me closer.

When he pulled away, his face crumpled with his own misery.

Scrutinizing the field, an unmarked grave, I realized it wasn't the same one where we buried Lola, the one I thought held Spencer's body. "How many killing fields do you lizards have?" I gasped.

Besides the obvious emotional pain Puma reflected, he repeated, "Lizards," as if I had just wounded him deeper with that remark. He sniffed and closed the gap between us. The man cried as he cupped my face with his hands.

"Your brother killed my brother," he said with a firm shake.

"W-what?"

He nodded hugely and let go. "Your brother," he said with cold aberration, "killed...*my* brother." His voice grew hoarse in a sort of subdued shout.

I trembled with disbelief.

"I will prove it to you. But now," he stopped crying as if on cue and wiped his eyes. "Make your peace with your brother." He flicked his chin toward the field.

"Where?" I gestured to the ground.

Puma paced a small area, tamped a patch of grassland with his brown shoe as if testing the density. "Here," he said. Then he sat in his car.

I lay down on my brother's grave and talked to him for a while. I said goodbye to Spencer, hoping he settled his forgotten account with the Lord before the ebb of his life faded completely. For good measure, I made sure he knew Mom, Dad, and I all love him and that...and that...I forgive him. Then I spoke with God, a song—that beloved hymn—pouring out from my soul.

Say, why in the valley of death should I weep, or alone in this wilderness rove? Oh why should I wander an alien from thee, and cry in the desert for bread? Thy foes will rejoice when my sorrows they see, and smile at the tears I have shed...

I stood then, and, spotting Puma through the windshield of the car, I witnessed behavior, verification, that he was no longer my foe.

We drove to *Agua de Dios* in silence, to Horacio's house. As evening set in, a beautiful ruby orange glow settled over the modest home in a modest town.

I welcomed the feeling of peace, almost forgetting about Horacio's promise to prove to me Spencer's—I didn't know what to call it—his *imperfections*.

He retrieved a hard case from a secured lockbox.

I sunk to the floor, sitting with legs crossed, on the cool brown tile between the kitchen and sofa area, which was one room, and waited.

Before Horacio unlocked the case, he said, "Your brother was a member of *Fuerzas Armadas Revolucionarias de Colombia—Ejército del Pueblo.* Do you now know about them?"

"Huh?"

"The Revolutionary..."

"...Armed Forces of Colombia," I said with him.

"People's Army," Horacio added. "He was not a mere lover of an affiliate; he belonged to the group."

"No way," I said emphatically. "Not my brother. He's not the type."

"It does not take a type, Sylvia, only a belief. Your brother was a Marxist." He nodded against my strong head wag. "*Sí.* FARC, one of the largest and oldest groups of its kind in South America, had ideals put in motion in nineteen forty-seven at a full assembly of the Colombian Communist Party, but was founded on May twentieth, nineteen sixty-four. They happen to hold particular esteem for Joseph Stalin. Interesting, uh?" he said with disdain. "Their socialistic ideology and their ethnically oppressive tactics crush my people." He snorted. "You think the paramilitary group to which I belong is the great evil, that I am the great evil." He tugged on his jaw. "*They* stipulate agrarian reform, these leftist insurgents who pit civil war, but they *force* farmers to take up their leftist causes. There are rarely volunteers. Not to mention, they justify the kidnapping of foreigners—a lot of them—demanding ransom to pay for their group's persistence. They are drug dealers and harvesters. FARC has an argument for everything, claiming they capture engineers who build dams, saying that it is for the good of ecology they do this, and for protecting Indian habitat. Only, in some areas, they practice ethnic separatism. Colombians, we are one." Horacio said proudly.

"Horacio…"

"Listen to me," he said. "The members of FARC murder 'enemies of the revolution.' If you are not *with* them, fighting alongside of them, you are their enemy."

"No, I don't think so. I've been to one of their camps. I met one of their commanders, Vasco. He was nice. I'm not one of them, yet he behaved like a true gentleman."

Horacio chewed on what I had pointed out. "So you've been to one of their camps?"

"I guess," I shrugged. "How many do they have?"

He inhaled. "The joint chiefs of staff manages their affairs in the eastern mountain range, southeast of Bogotá. They have many mobile headquarters, as well as some stationary." Horacio paused. "Well, Vasco wants something from you then."

"Like what?"

"My head, on a platter, uh? Corroborating with the human rights groups…" Horacio contemplated. "They are in communication with some of these groups to attempt a fair exchange for those they kidnapped for ransom. However, FARC has been known to deliver a cadaver instead of a live person after collecting payoff. It is a kind of joke to them, you know?"

I huffed. "There is nothing funny about this."

Horacio gazed at me. "They have a death squad. Factions in nearly every region in the country are sent to carry out terrorist attacks on innocent citizens ongoing. FARC is always at work. Their purposed actions took my brother's life. They also ambushed a military convoy and murdered my best friend—gunned him down—in two thousand eight. Brutality breeds brutality. It takes trained soldiers, police, military and paramilitary, to combat these dissidents. If we didn't react, FARC would run the country into the ground. Colombians as a whole are an exuberant, life-loving people, Sylvia."

"I know," I said with longing.

"These guerrillas, they have a way of suppressing life, instilling fear, jeopardizing safety, terrorizing people."

I rubbed my eyes, exhaustion setting in. "Can we get back to my brother?"

Horacio ruffled his hair with impatience. "He operated under the name *Evaristo*."

"Who?"

"Your brother," he arced his arm with irritated exaggeration. "They also called him *Flaco* ...it means thin, skinny."

My head dropped. I didn't think I wanted to hear any more.

"I assure you he was a Marxist who was involved in armed conflicts and carried out violent tactics."

"No! We weren't raised that way."

"That makes no difference. What is truth is truth. Here," he proceeded to pull out photographs. "His girlfriend, Ana Delarosa de Vélez, is an organizer for Fifty-fifth front. Evaristo—Spencer—was a member of the urban militia. Here, look at the photographs."

"No."

Horacio sighed. "In the past year alone, the Fifty-fifth claimed three bomb threats. Two at the U.S. embassy. One was false, the other we located the explosive in time. When a politician, a conservative and a supporter of former President Uribe, who often spoke out against leftist insurgents, held a public meeting outside of a hotel in La Candelaria district, a bomb—later claimed by FARC—detonated. It wounded thirteen and killed six. My brother, Pedro, also a member of National Police, was killed by that terrorist attack."

I studied the intensity in his face. "I'm sorry," I said.

He harrumphed. "Evaristo planted the bomb…"

"No," I shook my head.

"Your brother entered the plaza with a certain rucksack containing explosives. He set that pack down, sliding it behind a public trash receptacle in the vicinity of the crowd, and then he walked away from it, knowing it would detonate, knowing it would injure and kill people."

"NO."

"These photos are from a surveillance camera before the detonation. Nobody noticed your brother's presence."

I could believe that much.

"He slipped in, he slipped out," Horacio continued. "Others were caught up in live music, a band was playing, excitement was heightened. It happened under our noses, because we were alerted to a threat targeting the airport during the same time, and that would have caused greater harm, more damage. Our people were busy sniffing out the airport terminals and suitcases in what ended up a false alarm."

"But your brother was at the public meeting. Why didn't his squad stop it or even notice a large pack sitting there unaccompanied?"

Horacio shrugged. "A very bad mistake. They were not paying attention."

"This is all terrible, but I assure you Spencer was not involved."

"Here are the photos. Take them. See for yourself."

"No."

"It is him. Look at them."

"No." I couldn't.

Horacio stood and let the photos flutter around me. He crossed his arms. "You wanted the truth."

I opened my eyes and stared at my brother. I recognized the dark blue windbreaker he wore, the one I bought him for his birthday four years ago.

He carried the large rucksack; he slipped it behind the garbage bin before he pushed his glasses farther up on his face; he glanced over his shoulder, and he walked away.

There were other photos too. Several snapshots of him at different times in other places, looking like a regular pale, nerdy...*ninja*. I started to pick them up then, on some sort of adrenaline rush, my heart crushing with each one. It was as if I held a childhood Flip Book in my hands. A stealthy snapshot of scrawny Spencer dressed and armed for a skirmish, Spencer at a makeshift practicing range, some sort of training camp. Spencer posed like somebody who had finally found himself within the swarthy image of a superhero given the name Evaristo. Flaco.

My hands fell into my lap. I shut my eyes with a gasp, trying to breathe.

"You see?" I heard Horacio say.

"Get out! Get out!" I screamed at the top of my lungs.

Only minutes later, when I spied Horacio through the window standing very still in the middle of his courtyard garden did I realize I had kicked the man out of his own house.

I had never known more confusion than at that point.

Not realizing how long I sat in that numbed place, the shock started to wear off, but then another torrent of bitter tears came.

I felt a hand squeeze my shoulder. Horacio sunk to his knees and took me in his arms. We grasped each other's faces in some kind of desperate appeal.

"You killed my brother," I sobbed.

"Your brother killed my brother," Horacio matched.

When the moment leveled and emotions lulled, Horacio said, "I knew your brother, spoke with him. Before...you know..." He implied. "We had warned him several times. He still did this thing. After you arrived in Colombia at that time, we had just apprehended and interrogated your brother for the final time. He was stubborn."

I snorted, knowing the truth of that statement. He really did know my brother. Spencer's physical appearance gave the impression of weakness, but he was strong-willed.

"If we had done it, seized him sooner, innocent bystanders would still live today. Pedro would still live. We have to put a stop to terrorist activities, Sylvia. Violence breeds violence."

I didn't want to admit it, yet I understood. "But why *me*," I whimpered. "I didn't do anything wrong."

At that, Puma's mouth quivered into a frown. "I am sorry," he pressed his forehead against mine and whispered, "please forgive me...forgive me." He swallowed hard. "We assumed you were involved because of the timing of your arrival to Bogotá. And, I admit, aside from what we tried to accomplish, although gruesome, personal feelings got in the way. I wanted to hurt you. Because of Pedro." He pulled away and stood with his hands on his hips, back turned to me. "When we realized you did not have a clue," he snorted, "the damage was already done. We did not know what to do with you then, a foreign citizen implicated in our fight against terrorism. It was easier to remove all traces of you, as if you never existed, never came to Colombia. A person sacrificed, maybe, for the good of the whole. We had to keep looking at the whole." He moved slightly and I saw his profile. I watched as he chewed on his words. "We could not send you back out into society."

"But you did."

"*Sí*. I did."

It was all too much.

"I'm tired," I mumbled.

He nodded and led me to a room with a bed. "There. Rest."

After I collapsed onto the mattress, the hinges squeaking in protest, I heard the door shut. At first, I didn't know if I could actually sleep. *O Thou in Whose Presence* I think permanently burned in my mind—I had dwelled on it so much in the past few months. I hummed.

He looks, and ten thousands of angels rejoice, and myriads wait for his word. He speaks, and eternity, filled with his voice, re-echoes the praise of the Lord.

A strange calm settled over me and I slept deeply for the first time in a long while.

Twenty-seven
A Life Lost, a Life Saved

Dear Shepherd, I hear, and will follow thy call. I know the sweet sound of thy voice. Restore and defend me, for thou art my all, and in thee I will ever rejoice...

A savory smell filled the room. I opened my eyes and wiped the crust from their lids. It took me a few minutes, but after I gained equilibrium, I ventured out of the bedroom and into the kitchen/living area.

"Morning," I said.

Horacio wheeled around with a spoon in his hand. "You mean *afternoon*." He delivered a rare smile.

"Seriously?"

"*Sí*," he said, lightly. "You have slept long. I am glad for you."

"It smells really good, what are you making?"

"*Ajiaco*."

I huffed. "I hate *ajiaco*."

"Ah, but you have not tried mine. It is the best. But it needs to simmer longer. Sit." He motioned to a chair at the nearby table.

Horacio set a cup of coffee in front of me.

"I need to contact Laura and let her know I'm okay."

"I have taken care of that for you."

"What do you mean?" I stared at him, alarmed.

"Relax," he smiled again. "I have called her."

"You *talked* to her...?"

"*Sí.*"

"I don't get it."

"Communication is necessary between enemies."

"She's not a member of FARC, is she?"

"No, but she's in love with one of their relationally uncommitted commanders," he chuckled.

I took a couple sips of the nutty tasting coffee. "Well, you're in a good mood," I mumbled over the rim. "What did you tell her?"

"That you were sleeping." Horacio tapped the spoon against the side of the stockpot.

"Ugh, I'm sure that conjured up particular images in her head. She has preconceived notions, you know."

"Indeed, I clarified the situation to her, and I gave her my word you were only sleeping, nothing more."

"And she believed you?"

"I let her listen to you snore. She said it was unmistakable."

"Oh, very funny!" I threw a rolled up magazine at him, which he caught and pointed playfully at me.

"Come, let us take a stroll."

"What about the *ajiaco*, you're just going to leave it unattended?"

"It will be fine. It is at a low temperature and it will simmer. When we return it should be ready then.

I took another sip of my coffee.

"You can bring that with you if you like." Horacio gestured to my cup.

I shrugged. "Sure, why not?"

We started to amble down the various streets in town, me complete with a coffee cup in my hand.

When we passed the church, I said to him, "So, you're a Christian?"

His shoulders rose and fell with a sigh. "*Sí.* I have not always lived it, you know, but my mother made sure I knew of Jesus while growing up. And not in the religious sense, but like, uh, a relationship. Personal, you know?"

I nodded.

"I was convicted by what happened to you, Sylvia."

"Just to me?"

He noisily sucked in air through his nose. "No. Our fight against terrorism is necessary, but it can get gruesome."

"Isn't there another way, I mean, what about talking it over, like you admitted you've proceeded with Laura?"

"Diplomacy does not always work. Yet, I have struggled with moral questions, my part in this conflict."

"But you don't stop."

He stretched his face. "It is what I have had to do."

We jumped back when a splash of water claimed our feet. An elderly man with a sweet prune face irrigated the flowerbox at his windowsill. He apologized, and then offered to refill my cup, gesturing humorously. The three of us laughed, and Horacio and I continued on our walk.

I gazed up at the sky and noted the gorgeous cloud formation, patterned like a mosaic.

"So your heart was convicted?"

"*Sí.* You know, one tries not to get personally involved. Instead, you rely on your exercise." He raised his brows, searching my face to see if I understood his intention. "I would not have stepped in, but I held so much hatred for you because I thought you were partly responsible for Pedro's death."

"Who would allow that, your stepping in? What boss, anyway, knowing your personal involvement and all?"

"Nazario."

"Frick?"

"*Sí.*"

"He's not normal."

Horacio cocked his head to the side. "Agreed. He is sick in the head, a pervert. I do not like working for him. He takes pleasure in the spoil of others. Especially women."

"And you don't?"

"No." His mouth opened and closed a few times as if considering his words. "Even when I hated you, it brought me no pleasure to hurt you. In fact, it made me despise myself, which caused me to despise you even more. Resentment grew, I suppose. And then..."

"And then?"

"God began convicting me. I realized soon enough that you were ignorant of the political climate in Colombia. You were just, uh, an innocent sister who had come to visit her beloved brother. It took time, but my feeling shifted from hatred to...prayer," he said, in the tone of a question.

The coffee cup, long empty, dangled off my finger against my leg. I stared at each crack in the pavement.

He continued, "I prayed that somehow, your life would be spared. That you and I could live the lives out fully what our brothers could not. I rededicated my own journey in the Lord, asked for his forgiveness. Begged for his guidance..."

"And you disobeyed orders...*Frick's*...to save me."

"Yes."

"Does anybody know? Nazario?"

He shrugged. *"No sé."*

"What will happen?"

He splayed his hands in an, *I don't know* gesture. "I am not sure it matters at this point. Aguilera's group will help bring about trials, I am certain. You are now here again. What to do?"

"We will trust the Lord, I guess." Did I just say that? Puma and I had come to a peculiar understanding of each other. In an odd way, I guess that put us on the same side. "You know, Horacio…"

"I like much better when you call me Horacio," he interrupted with a smile.

"Yeah," I said quietly.

"No more addressing me as Puma, okay?"

"Okay."

He waited for me to finish.

"You know…well, I know you know," I rambled. "I was sick a lot at The Water Cave. In my greatest mental and physical suffering, and even while doped up after my visit to the infirmary, I felt Jesus was asking something of me. Through it all, he asked me to pray for my enemies." I stopped and faced him. "You were my enemy. I hated you the most. You were all the prisoners' favorite, because they thought you exhibited the most moral confliction. They considered you the most gentle. Yet, you shredded every ounce of me until there was nothing left."

He flinched and looked away.

"But I-I started reciting a scripture I memorized as a child, to love my enemy, to pray for my persecutors, that God, Jesus, send his rain down on both the good and the evil. It has taken time, but I prayed for you. And I forgive you, Horacio, I forgive you."

When he faced me, his expression said it all. His eyes filled but didn't spill. He stretched his mouth and nodded his timeless thanks.

Without a prompt, we reinitiated our stroll.

Twenty-eight
Things Are Never What They Seem

From the opposite direction, the street started to look familiar, and his home came into view. In the breezeway, I said, "You have a nice house."

"It belonged to my brother." Horacio opened the door and motioned for me to enter. The seasoned aroma of stew wrapped its flavorful tendrils around me, rousing my stomach to greater hunger.

"Sit. We will eat."

Apparently, he had forgotten my earlier anti-*ajiaco* comment.

When he placed a bowl under my nose and sat across from me with his own, I felt his scrutiny but I couldn't take my eyes off the potpourri of ingredients. I stared at it and summed up Colombia in that one bowl.

Horacio's gentle voice washed over me from across the table. "You will not hate it once you have tried mine. It is the best. Trust me."

"I don't really hate it," I sniffed. "I love *ajiaco*." Tears dripped off my chin into the soup, adding more salt to the mix.

I thought Horacio offered a box of Kleenex, but when I glanced up, he was extending a plate of *arepas*, which I declined. He shrugged. I got lost in thought.

My brother wasn't who I thought he was. I don't know when the change occurred. I suppose I noticed it a few years before he left for Colombia. I'd say that an inner fear of losing him completely instigated the impromptu visit to Bogotá that drastically changed my life. However, the story had much more personal substance. I suppose, in a way, Colombia drew me in. I had wanted a different life. Witnessing my older brother move overseas and settling within another culture gave me the same desire to do something similar. I just didn't know how to do it. Maybe I was afraid to step out. I had hoped Spencer would desire the same thing for me, would aid me in moving, or exhibit enthusiasm. I had no idea of his involvement with a left wing terrorist group. He turned his back on his family, his beliefs, and his roots, those things that made him who he was.

I yearned for a new life, a change of pace, of scenery. I got it, but it turned out differently than I had expected. Still, I am the same person. After torture, I thought I lost the essence of *me*. Instead, I realize I am actually finding it by discovering more of God. I grew to know the Lord at a deeper level than I have ever known by praying for my enemy. It only turns out that my enemy isn't what I thought either. Outside prison walls and "operating theaters"—and even within—Horacio was a human being with faults, emotions, weaknesses, shortcomings, just like me. Just like the rest of us.

How do you combat terrorists without the potential use of unscrupulous measures?

I don't know. I'll leave that for others to decide. I only happened to get caught in the cross hairs. The one thing I do know, God is in control. Sometimes he allows bad things to happen. But I know...*that in all things God works for the good of those who love him, who have been called according to his purpose.* We are more than conquerors.

That last line I must have uttered aloud, for Horacio answered me and said, "*Sí*, more than conquerors..." He bit into an *arepa*.

I lifted a spoonful of *ajiaco* into my mouth and just about fell over; it tasted so delicious.

"Yum, Horacio," I pointed to my mouth as I chewed in ecstasy.

"You like," he delivered a broad smile. "I told you, it is the best!"

He tried to offer me *arepas* again.

This time, I grabbed one. "I love Colombia."

He set the plate down and shrugged. "What is there not to love?"

Twenty-nine
The Quintessence of Life

"Horacio, what's next?"

We lounged on the sofa. The dessert plates on the coffee table we had pushed away only moments ago held *Postre de Natas*—a sweet, Christmas pudding, as Horacio explained, that he favored often and preferred to prepare thick enough to slice into squares. A few raisins remained, spotting my dish. Without a second thought, I leaned over and gathered them, popping them into my mouth.

"I would like to open my own restaurant someday."

Glancing at the dessert plates again, chewing, I laughed. "It would be packed every night." Then I shifted toward him. "But I mean now...what's going to happen now?"

"I do not know. I suppose we will wait and see."

"We?"

He motioned his head back and forth as if deciding on sentence structure. "I feel a sense to take care of you. I do not know, maybe you belong in Colombia, uh?" He met my gaze.

"I want to stay in Colombia," I affirmed.

"You may need to change your name. Sylvia is acceptable, but we may need to come up with an alternate surname. For your protection," he jested.

"For my protection, huh?" I smiled. "Horacio, what do you think is the embodiment of life?"

He breathed deeply, "The embodiment of life is to keep living and while we live, to forgive. Jesus is life. The rest," he waved his hand, "is unessential in the end. He is what we live for and our only..." he searched for words.

"Salve," I offered.

"*Sí*. Our only salve. It often is a cruel world, uh?"

"Yeah. Man's sin fully unleashed. I'm grateful, Horacio, that Jesus didn't forget about me," I said in the stillness of the darkened room. "But I wonder about the others, like my brother. Did he make peace with God before he died?"

I suppose I asked the question hoping Horacio would assure me Spencer did. However, when he tensed and glanced away, I knew Spencer probably kicked and cursed his journey out of this life, and kept his back turned on the one who offered eternal salvation. It takes but a second to cross from one form of life to the next. My brother had long ago snubbed faith. Did he really know it at all? My heart constricts as I ponder such things.

Be ready always...

I heard the admonition resound in my mind.

"So!" Horacio said. "I like to cook. I am a chef. You are a marketer. When I finish my term with the National Police, what shall we call our new restaurant?"

"Puma's Purgatory?"

He pinched the bridge of his nose. "Life Sylvia, think new life! The old is over and done."

I moaned in contemplation. "Abbott and Botello."

He snickered with impatience. "I think you meant Abbott and Costello. And you pronounced it wrong." Horacio nudged me. "We have time to decide, but not right now. Service begins in a few minutes."

"Service?" I asked.

"Church. Down the street. Unless you are opposed to worshipping together?" He stood and paused.

"I suppose if we've been through hell together, found saving grace together, and are going to open a new restaurant together, then we probably ought to worship together."

Horacio smirked.

We had trekked through the valley of the shadow of death, each in our own way. On the other side, we found goodness and restoration, comfort, the fragrance of life— forgiveness. Now we will dwell, yes my torturer and I, in the house of the Lord forever. Who could imagine such an unspeakable thing?

Smiling, I clasped the hand Horacio offered and found my feet.

"This righteousness from God comes through faith in Jesus Christ to all who believe. There is no difference, for all have sinned and fall short of the glory of God, and are justified freely by his grace through redemption that came by Christ Jesus."

Romans 3:22-24

"La justicia de Dios por medio de la fe en Jesucristo, para todos los que creen en él. Porque no hay diferencia, por cuanto todos pecaron, y están destituidos de la gloria de Dios, siendo justificados gratuitamente por su gracia, mediante la redención que es en Cristo Jesús."

Romanos 3:22-24

Meet

Tessa Stockton

A veteran of the performing arts and worldwide missions, Tessa Stockton also contributed as a writer/editor for ministry publications, ghostwriter for political content, and she headed a column on the topic of forgiveness. Today she writes novels in a variety of genres, often laced with romance and intrigue. In addition to her suspense/thriller, THE UNSPEAKABLE, she's the author of the political intrigue/romance novel, THE UNFORGIVABLE, a literary short story, LOVE AND LULL, and the upcoming inspirational fantasy romance, WIND'S ARIA, with more in the works. Visit her at www.TessaStockton.com

VISIT OUR WEBSITE
FOR THE FULL INVENTORY
OF QUALITY BOOKS:

http://www.wings-press.com

Quality trade paperbacks and downloads
in multiple formats,
in genres ranging from light romantic
comedy to general fiction and horror.
Wings has something
for every reader's taste.
Visit the website, then bookmark it.
We add new titles each month!